SIMPSON RETURNS

WAYNE MACAULEY

TEXT PUBLISHING MELBOURNE AUSTRALIA

textpublishing.com.au

The Text Publishing Company
Swann House
22 William Street
Melbourne Victoria 3000
Australia

Published by The Text Publishing Company, 2019

Cover design by Design by Committee
Page design by Text
Typeset by J&M Typesetting

Printed and bound in Australia by Griffin Press, an accredited ISO/NZS 14001:2004 Environmental Management System printer

ISBN: 9781925773507 (paperback)
ISBN: 9781925774313 (ebook)

A catalogue record for this book is available from the National Library of Australia.

This book is printed on paper certified against the Forest Stewardship Council® Standards. Griffin Press holds FSC chain-of-custody certification SGS-COC-005088. FSC promotes environmentally responsible, socially beneficial and economically viable management of the world's forests.

'Wayne Macauley is an Australian original. He writes in a tradition of dystopian satire—associated most famously with George Orwell's *1984* or Aldous Huxley's *Brave New World*—but in a stripped-back and absurdist style. His work is a mixture of Jonathan Swift, Samuel Beckett, Franz Kafka and J. M. Coetzee (in allegorical mode), though Macauley's fictional worlds are always set in Melbourne or greater Victoria. The meaning or relevance of his dystopian satires are to be found locally too, in our country's follies.'

Saturday Paper

'Macauley has published some of the most memorable fiction going in this country. His books and stories are satirical fables in which the properties are recognisably contemporary and Australian...His narratives [can] take off into the bizarre without ever losing their cool.'

Age

'He makes readers feel uncomfortable, unsettled in the everyday; one emerges from his books freshly uncertain.'

Lifted Brow

'Macauley has a nose for exposing the zeitgeist.'

Australian

'A writer always worth reading.'

Sydney Morning Herald

Wayne Macauley is the author of the acclaimed novels *Some Tests*, *Demons*, *The Cook*, *Caravan Story* and *Blueprints for a Barbed-Wire Canoe*. He has been shortlisted for a Victorian Premier's Literary Award (twice), a Western Australian Premier's Book Award, a Queensland Premier's Literary Award, the Melbourne Prize for Literature's Best Writing Award and an Adelaide Festival Award for Literature. He lives in Melbourne.

waynemacauley.com

For Graham Henderson,
who gave me the goad.

...lowly, and riding upon an ass...

ZECHARIAH 9:9

NOTE

The following events are assumed to have taken place over the course of roughly six weeks in the early part of 2003.

1

THE SITUATION EXPLAINED

I, Simpson, and my donkey, Murphy, eighty-eight years resurrected, are still on the road, still together, still looking for the Inland Sea. This trip looks like our last. Fair weather the barometer said, then two days out of Melbourne it rained. We were a little short of Diggers Rest, on the Toolern Vale road. It came upon us quickly, boiling black clouds on the western horizon and a great blast of wind from the south. Murphy got bogged in a roadside ditch and I could not get him out. He squawked, irascibly, each time I tugged at his rein and for one terrible moment I thought he was giving up on me and wanted to go home. But I got him out in the end. That night as he slept I saw the shiver coursing through his flanks and knew he had caught cold. The next day the shivering grew worse and small rivulets of green snot fell from Murphy's nostrils. I have plied him with all possible cures but he takes them reluctantly; since north of Crowlands I've carried the pannier bags myself. I still hope to make the Sunset Country before the summer ends—perhaps the dry air there will put him back on his feet? All the best laid plans.

He's a good animal, I can't deny it, a little on the mulish side at times but old enough for me to forgive him his irritating ways. We've been through a lot together, Murphy and I, but the beast has stuck by me where many other donkeys and no doubt many more humans would have given up years ago. He's from India, originally. What he thinks of our enterprise, I cannot say: not even I, his lifelong companion, can penetrate that inscrutable look. Perhaps he simply has nowhere else to go, nothing else to do: better a futile journey than a more futile staying at home. I've studied his face often these past few days for a sign of his present thinking but the look is more inscrutable than ever. Can anyone understand a donkey, what goes on in a donkey's mind? I am more qualified than most, but no wiser than a century ago.

This is our twenty-ninth attempt; the other twenty-eight, I don't mind saying, have been somewhat less than successful. We have never got out of the state of Victoria. Last time it was the wasps—Murphy has a fear of wasps, among other things, and in attempting to clear a path through them he caught my chin with his hoof. I could not eat for days. That was just past Burnside. Bad luck is often like bad weather, I find: one minute you're free of it, the next it's falling on top of your head. We returned again to Mrs Fowler's place in Richmond with our tails between our legs. Mrs Fowler's daughter asks no questions; the gate to the back lane is always open, as with her dear mother before her. When we wake in the morning fresh straw is waiting outside the stable door and a small breakfast has been prepared. Most of the stables in that street are gone now, converted to garages and studios, but ours has been kept more or less unchanged since the day we first moved in. It's comforting to know that blood ties still run deep and old debts are still dutifully discharged. Apparently I had done some good turn for the widow Fowler's husband: the man with the donkey, he said, in his last letter to her, be sure you repay the debt.

The daughter's name is June. Her husband suffers

me stoically. On my triennial visits 'home' he studiously avoids the backyard and lets his wife attend to our needs. Are the man and the donkey back again? he asks, looking out through the kitchen window with a smile. He doesn't see us, of course, but through her silences he reads our presence. I try to keep out of their way and do what I can not to overstay my welcome. She never fusses about us too much, though; it is enough for her that she keeps the promise, in deference to the father she never knew. She was conceived on the eve of Mr Fowler's sailing and is now in her eighty-ninth year. We are all getting old. If this trip should somehow prove successful I hope she will be the first to profit from it.

I wasn't always looking for the Inland Sea. Helpmate to the dying, that was the lot I was burdened with and one which (with no false modesty) brought me some measure of fame and a steady supply of good-quality cigarettes in those earlier, far-off days. I still wear the Red Cross armband, threadbare now with age. We brought the bloodied racks of bodies back to the hospital tent, drank what little hospital brandy we could find, then journeyed out into the terrible cacophony again. A man and his donkey. I have a photograph of us somewhere, in my pannier bags I think: me a rough-headed youth smiling a smile that could almost be a grimace, Murphy looking disdainfully for God knows what reason at my foot. That was the Great War, they called it the Great War, and I'm sure it was great for some, but somehow the greatness of it got past Murphy and me and we had to content ourselves with the trivialities of blood and broken limbs.

Then one day down at the clearing station a few weeks in a wounded soldier with half his guts missing called me over to his bed. Lasseter was his name. He said he'd heard of the work I was doing, that I was the one man here who could not afford to be lost. From inside his pocket he took out a vial, a small glass vial, with a clear liquid, water, inside. Rub a little on your forehead, he said, if ever you get in trouble—I could use it myself but I'm past caring, I've seen enough these last few days to know that life is not worth living. A good man. I hung the vial on a string around my neck and set off into the maelstrom again. When I came back later that day, Lasseter's stretcher was empty.

Yes, they were strange days, the days of war. If they taught us nothing else they taught us that hate does not get you far in this world. All those boys, they all hated as best they could, sent hatred down the barrels of their guns in the direction of Johnny Turk, but for all their hating they could not win, they would not win, they were still losers, they lost. From their tents on the beaches the generals barked and asked couldn't we smell that stinking paprika and garlic coming off those filthy Ottomans and didn't we want to drive our bayonets through their dirty olive skins—yet we could smell nothing but our own cordite and blood. I walked through Johnny Turk's hell-fire, asking to be hit. I believed the meek would inherit the earth, no matter what state the earth was in once the unmeek had finished with it. I stood for crucifixion, the others for rough Roman justice. One morning on my way back down Shrapnel Gully I took a sniper's bullet through the heart. I lay where I fell, gazing up at Murphy braying, until in the blind panic that only death's nearness can bring I uncorked the vial and took a swig.

I awoke three days later in a hospital ship on my way to the island of Lemnos; Murphy, they said, was safely below. The padre stroked his chin: this was something outside his parish. I pleaded with him not to send us back—I'll make a better hero back home, I said, if they hear I was killed in action. The padre creased his forehead. He wasn't going to believe in the Resurrection, not this time round anyway, it would only give him trouble in the long run. He would try to bury us, if not actually then figuratively, and move on to other things. When we docked at Lemnos he got a job for us carting water for the monks in the monastery up on the hill. For this we got bread, wine and board and a life of which few ex-servicemen could boast, and in this Aegean idyll we lived out the final years of the war while over on the Peninsula the blood of thousands stained the dirt.

We came home at war's end on the steamer *Medic* and docked at Melbourne, where the Spanish influenza pandemic was at that time raging. I begged some work from the Sisters of Mercy, carting influenza victims from the backstreet slums at tuppence on delivery, but truth to say my heart wasn't really in it. I had lost the necessary compassion, I think, to return to my old line of work.

And the Inland Sea? What drove me to that? I who could have lived untroubled with Murphy in that warm stable in Richmond until the last gene in the Fowler line was extinguished? I never really knew what happened that day in Shrapnel Gully, except that age had not seemed to weary me since, nor it seemed my donkey. Then one morning in the kitchen, shortly after our arrival, the widow Fowler cut her finger. In taking her hand to look at the damage I must have brushed against the wound. The bleeding stopped, and the cut closed over. A miracle—it was only then that I grasped the full extent of the vial's power. The news spread, and for the next few years I paid my way, performing little healing tricks for those who sought me out. Only those who believed were cured, for it was only those who believed who could be certain of my existence. My cures were not grand by any means—I could close a cut finger or turn back a common cold—and my fees were correspondingly small. But I had landed on my feet, and while all the returned soldiers wandered the streets of Melbourne, prematurely aged, with the spectre of death and suffering in their eyes, I slept snug and warm in Mrs Fowler's stable with barely a grey hair on my head.

Then one day in the summer of 1928, a man came knocking on my door. A sick-looking man, pale and wasted, with a hunted look in his eye. It was Lasseter, the wounded soldier. He'd survived, minus most of his intestine and bowel. I could do nothing for him. But didn't I still have the vial? he asked. I'd kept it, of course, on the string around my neck, but the contents were long since gone. It's here, I said, pulling it out. But the water, he asked, the water inside? I turned to Murphy; Murphy bowed his head. I looked at the ceiling, then bowed my head too. Lasseter held his in his hands.

Seventy-five years: it's a long time looking, by anyone's estimation. Lasseter is long since dead. But as Mrs Fowler dispatched her duty to me so I will mine to him. Don't worry, I had said (how easily said!), I will fill the vial again. He gave me the map with the details on it but I have trouble reading it now. My eyesight is failing, my bones have started to creak, my healing powers are not what they were. But if twenty-eight failed attempts so far have given us little cause for optimism, still, we must go on. We follow the vast network of fissures and gullies inland, leaning on charity where we must, paying our way where we can. In the pannier bags I carry herbs, plant extracts, dried animal parts, healing stones, all the little tricks I've picked up along the way. In the vial I keep an Ayurvedic gem, the locust egg that a Talmudist gave me, a sliver of deer's antler that I got from a Chinese. I draw on the haberdashery of knowledge I have accumulated, from people I've talked to and books I've read, and fill in the gaps extempore. I mark my face and utter ritual incantations of my own invention; I crush crusty snail shells with a mortar and pestle and keep the dust in a Vegemite jar. But the physician cannot heal himself. My bones are cold in the marrow, my heart speaks to me out of tune. I go to the memorials where the heave offerings are left: tinned food, biscuits, brandy, cigarettes. I stand at the back door of a country pub at closing time and beg for a bottle and a carrot for Murphy: Lest we forget, I say. The farmers dutifully whip around among themselves and the publican returns with my booty wrapped up in a brown paper bag. I accept it graciously—You will be blessed with many children, I say, in the fullness of time—and disappear again into the night to rejoin Murphy at our camp on the outskirts where beside a fire of broken fence palings and pallets I drink. Murphy says nothing, but behind his supposedly vacant eyes I'm sure I see a look of reproach. We are on our way to the Sunset Country, I say, then north, to the Inland Sea. But he is little reassured. He stands removed, chewing on his withered carrot, his eyes deliberately averted to the ground. By God he is an obstinate beast.

2

THE RUINED WOMAN

We left Fowlers' that early March morning with the barometer fair and the wind from the north, skirted the city on the river side and crossed the Maribyrnong by Shepherd Bridge. Through the bluestone lanes of Footscray and out into the wilds of Footscray West my plan was, as always (my twenty-ninth attempt!), to pick up the Kororoit Creek past Brooklyn and let it guide us windingly north across the black soil plains.

We made first camp as evening fell behind the tennis courts in Deer Park. The plaque there is set in a basalt boulder on a patch of lawn under a tree, a favourite stopping place. The locals here are mostly kind. In the lee of the rock they had left a can of baked beans, one of pressed meat and six miniature bottles of Remy. This is where last trip I cured the young addict Ekrem Bata: estranged from his parents, truant from school, no job and no government help, he had been robbing houses until one day in an insensible state he'd left his girlfriend inside and run. She was given a bond but would have no more to do with the traitor. Ekrem went downhill. I found him shivering under a streetlight; the park was otherwise quiet. Oh Jack, he said. His eyes when I first pulled back the lids looked to have closed their apertures forever: they would admit light no more. But look and you will see something stirring: a flicker of life, a hint of goodness, of something sadly lost. Are you all right? I asked. Hmvsh, said Ekrem Bata. Take this and put it over you, I said. I removed that other, disingenuous blanket, and replaced it with the warm blanket of love. To the plaza or your girlfriend's? My girlfriend's, please, said Ekrem Bata. I whistled Murphy up. The going was easy. Along the way I administered my potions, softened the hard edges of his horrors with a velvet poultice to the heart. We halted on the footpath outside his girlfriend's house in Sunshine. His bowels loosened by all this exercise, Murphy decided now was the time to shit. Go, I said: Be brave. I watched Ekrem walk up the drive. The girlfriend answered, and in an instant she had draped his neck and shoulders with her arms.

I collected my things from the lee of the rock, tethered Murphy where he could get at the grass, and in the gathering darkness I opened and ate the beans. Later that evening a boy came by on a bike and held out a hamper for me. It's from me dad, he said. His hand was trembling: the kid's father had warned him what to expect but I was still a frightful sight. The one who fell off the scaffold, he said. Ah yes, I said, remembering—I wanted to talk, the wisdom of the ancients, but the frightened boy was already gone.

All went quiet then, save for the cars out on Station Road and, further off, the highway. It's my lot to be set apart. In the days of my Great War heroics I never got any further than that tangle of gullies just beyond the beachhead, in my travels since no further than the dry creek beds and back roads of country Victoria. Will I always move in the hollows, the defiles and ravines? But even on my bad days I still see it, this Inland Sea of mine, its shimmering surface, its unfathomable depths, and can feel it drawing me to its bosom. It will let me in, I think, like from where Adam and Eve were put out; the gates will open, music will play and riding Murphy regally I will come into its care. Food and wine will be offered, great tables laid. And it will not just be me who enjoys this banquet, no, but all those who have laboured on the margins, crawled in the lowlands, been cast out and abused. All these I will let sit at my table, all these will be my guests; there will be chops and sausages, vegetarian hamburgers too, great piles of mashed potato there will be, tomato sauce and cans of peas; there will be bread and dips; pizza we will have and pastas of every sort; all halal meats we will eat, bled and tender and lean; we will eat sweet-and-sour pork and rice-paper rolls; green curries and red curries, hot and mild; all this will be ours and we will eat it together as one big family under one big sky.

The next morning, with Murphy hobbling like the geriatric ass that he is, we resumed our journey through Deer Park and St Albans—car wrecks, shredded rubbish, in places great crops of plastic tree-protectors stretching out across both banks like the tombstones of the fallen—and around the back of Caroline Springs towards Leakes Road north of Rockbank. From there I planned to lunch at the memorial in the picturesque town of Toolern Vale, cross the perilous Lerderderg Gorge north of Bacchus

Marsh and take the snaking gully inland.

I felt purposeful in my step, if not sprightly; aside from a few swallowtail clouds the heaven above was spread with blue. Then I saw a red hatchback, parked on the gravel verge. It was hard to tell from that distance (despite the comfrey compresses I put on my poor eyes every night) whether what I saw rocking back and forward inside was a head or a headrest. But as we got closer it became clear to me that behind the wheel of that four-door runabout was a soul at the end of its tether. I tied Murphy to the fence and tapped on the window. Are you all right? I asked.

Not everyone sees me—it just depends. I am Old Truth, Enduring Myth, Simple Hope, Unfashionable Kindness. If you do not need me, you will not see me. Shelley Jaecks looked around. Pitiable sight! Cheeks streaked with tears, eyes red and make-up smudged, a snotty nose. She would have been an attractive woman once, had not the ravages of poverty and time marked her face. She was in her late thirties, at most. With flibberty fingers she lifted the sodden ball of tissues from her lap and dabbed her poor nose with it. I opened the door and climbed into the passenger seat. It smelled of cigarettes and pine forests. Shelley had seen me and could no longer deny I was there—old schooldays Simpson, whose story crackled out of the cassette deck every anniversary afternoon and whose likeness could be followed in the picture book the teacher then held up to the class. Selfless Simpson the Saviour, giving comfort to the injured on his egalitarian ass. Shelley and I both stared out the windscreen. In the back seat her three children slept. There was a sadness in the car like slow-falling rain. Tell me your story, I said.

She had tried to attach a length of hose to the exhaust pipe—she'd seen it done this way in the movies and could not understand why the hose wouldn't fit. Making fine incisions around its circumference didn't make it any easier, nor the fifty-millimetre duct tape she went back to Sunbury to buy. She'd given the children something to make them sleep and spent ages trying to get the thing to work—but every time she turned the key the hose popped off. In the end with a thousand curses she hurled it all from her. She got back in the car, put her head on the steering wheel and wept.

Her husband had left her. A store manager in a furniture warehouse, he had taken up with one of his employees, a blond-haired woman called Belinda, herself recently divorced. Each week he dropped off a little cash and a note for the kids in an envelope slipped under the door. He thought this would keep things quiet, and for a time it had, until Shelley casually mentioned this arrangement one morning to one of the school mothers outside the school gate. No, said the school mother, definitely not, this wasn't right, her husband should pay her more and she should speak to someone about it.

Later that week Shelley found herself sitting opposite a social-welfare advocate: a tall, well-built woman in a loose-fitting cotton dress with fashionably cut grey hair. Around the walls of her office were posters of rainforests and colour snaps of herself hiking in them. The woman asked how she could help. Shelley stumbled over her words at first—she found it difficult to talk about money—then shaped a few sentences that seemed to explain the situation. But I don't mind, she said; I can manage. The woman moved some things around on her desk, then moved them back again. Well, she said, Shelley, there *are* strict rules in this country governing spousal maintenance—not to mention the fact that as a single mother you are entitled to a separate fortnightly payment. Are you keeping a diary?

Shelley didn't understand and asked did she mean of her feelings? The woman smiled and said no, her schedule. She took some booklets from the drawer, and, using them to explain what she called the *child-support percentage* and the *basic formula*, roughly calculated her husband's financial obligations to her. She slid the piece of paper across the desk. Shelley could see the sweat marks left by her hands. These figures are estimates only, said the woman, but if I were you I would quickly find a way of formalising these payments, in the interests of both yourself and the children.

Shortly after this conversation, Shelley rang her estranged husband and asked him to raise his support payments from the modest sum he was paying to a minimum of three hundred dollars a week. He told her to get stuffed and if she wanted he'd see her in court. Shelley was going to explain the *basic formula* to him but then he hung up.

Shelley Jaecks held out as long as she could. She tightened the belt at home and made the kids go without. She delayed her bill-paying. She rang her parents for help—they had never been close—but they just gave her the usual lecture about standing on her own two feet. Eventually she made an appointment with a lawyer recommended to her by the social-welfare woman; Garrison Moore sent her home with some brochures and forms and told her to make another appointment with his secretary for the following week. She left feeling good about herself again, but when she got home she found a disconnection notice from the electricity company, a final notice on the telephone and another reminder about her credit card. The following day, more disconcertingly, she received a package from the lawyer outlining his exorbitant rates and the costs she had already incurred. After putting the children to bed, Shelley drank the cask of red wine she'd bought the previous day and chain-smoked the cigarettes she could no longer afford to buy. The next day she rang the lawyer and explained how she couldn't afford to pay; she was sorry, she would have to drop the case. But then in what Shelley tragically believed was a suggestive tone of voice Garrison Moore said not to worry, it was fine, they could 'make arrangements' and she should come to his office the next day to discuss it.

Shelley knew she was walking into something she would regret. But what else was she to do? She had three kids to support, a household to run. She put on her best dress, her best lipstick, put up her hair and dabbed herself with perfume. Outside Garrison Moore's office she had one last nervous cigarette and popped a mint in her mouth.

The thing is, said the lawyer, annoyingly clicking the end of his pen, your case is nothing unusual, I see this kind of thing all the time. The courts are clogged with them. I blame the times we live in, the messages we're getting from people in high places who should know better; we're encouraged not to care for others—I mean, human beings are like that anyway, they don't need extra encouragement from above. He smiled. You have a strong case to force your husband to pay child support, it is entirely appropriate that he does, but I suspect he won't think he has to until the judge tells him otherwise. So it is our job to get this case before a judge as soon as possible and present to him or her the facts.

Garrison Moore grabbed a couple of things from his drawer; he was working with an efficiency gained from years of experience, he could almost do it blind. So far he had barely looked at Shelley, instead addressing various objects around the room: the potted plant, the framed certificate, the spare chair in the corner. So what I'll need from you, Shelley, he continued, are just a few specific incidents where your husband has failed to provide. He placed the pen very carefully on the desk in front of him and waited for her to speak.

Shelley had been listening, but only with one ear. With the other she was listening to the inside of her head which was telling her that she couldn't wait, that it was up to her now, that all this talk from the lawyer was just evasion; the only reason he wasn't looking at her was so she could say (and say quickly) what she had to say without embarrassment. About the payment, she said, with a slight stammer. She leaned towards him: Would you take something other than money? Of course the lawyer looked at the dark crevice there, but he didn't look for long. He quickly chose another object in the room to give his focus to. Shelley slid one finger around the scooped neck of her dress, forcing it open a few millimetres more, and leaned a little further forward. She felt ridiculous, she'd never done anything like this before; her cleavage, ruined by three merciless mouths, was not even worth showing. I'm happy to give you what you want, she said, if you can help me: I'm mortgaged to the eyeballs, nothing's paid for, everything's on credit. You've got to help. Shelley's eyes were glistening. I'll do anything, she said.

Garrison Moore finally looked at her. He was calm,

as he always was when a client out of nowhere revealed their darker side to him. Mrs Jaecks, he said, please, thank you for your offer but I don't think I'm the lawyer for you: we'll end our session there if you don't mind. Good luck, I hope you find someone who will help. No! said Shelley. Please, I'll do anything! There's nothing you can do, said the lawyer. He was on his feet now; he moved away from the desk and took up a position between it and the door. Please, he said. Shelley stood up. Garrison Moore put his hand on the doorhandle and opened it. From her desk in reception his secretary turned and looked in. You'll have to go, said the lawyer. Now exposed to witnesses, helpless, humiliated, Shelley Jaecks had no choice. She picked up her handbag and left.

The lawyer's office was behind the main street, in one of those mini-malls that through an arcade opens out onto a wide, white-lit space surrounded by cafés and shops. Shelley bought a coffee and a doughnut, found a spare table and sat. She could feel her life going off the rails, could feel inside a clunk and screech as of a train leaving its tracks. There was a local paper lying on the table; she pulled it towards her and flicked through it and stopped at a page near the back.

*

I'm hungry, Mum, said one of the kids. We're starving, Mum, said another. They were all waking up. Shh, said Shelley Jaecks. What are we doing here? they said. I'm talking to the man with the donkey, said their mother. The boys all looked out the window. Can we ride him? they asked. Not now, said Shelley. They can ride him if they want, I said.

From out of my pannier bags I distributed some cheese crackers. Let them stretch their legs for a while, I said, the fresh air will do them good. We all stood by the side of the road. It was very quiet. There were paddocks either side, dry but for a scattering of green weeds, the one on the left rising up gradually to the top of Mount Kororoit, formerly Mount Misery, more a hill than a mountain really, and from the top of which rose a telephone tower. Murphy stood tethered to a fencepost with a morose look on his face. Can we ride him, *please*? the children asked. What could their mother say? If her children could see my donkey (and, presumably, me) then they were as much a part of this strange conspiracy as she: we were all in it together. Yes, she said, but one at a time; and go carefully, please.

It was hard for them to go either one at a time or carefully, so much did these few words excite them. I put up a policeman's hand and asked for a moment's patience. I removed the pannier bags and hung them on the fence. I untethered Murphy and led him into the adjoining paddock. I gave the reins to Thomas and helped little Cooper aboard. Now you watch he holds on, I said to Jake, the other one: and if the donkey won't move you give him a poke. I gave him my favourite goad. Jake wasted no time in using it and Murphy bounced up into a trot. Cooper held on as best he could while Thomas ran alongside.

They seem happy enough, I said to Shelley. She wiped her eyes and nodded. Murphy himself seemed to have rediscovered a lost youth, in his mind perhaps trotting down the dusty backstreets of his ancestral village, the children chasing behind. Certainly I'd never seen such a lightness in his step. My beast seems happy too, I said.

Why did you stop? asked Shelley: You could have left me here to die. Inveterate Samaritanism, I said. But didn't you say you were on your way somewhere? she asked. I am, I said, as always: but I never seem to get there. Then shouldn't you stop stopping? she said—sensibly, I had to admit. But I can't stop stopping, I said. Then you'll never get there, she said. True, I said. We then watched the children for a while, skipping and stumbling as they followed a light-footed little-legged Murphy around the farmer's paddock.

The number that Shelley Jaecks had rung was the one in bold print in a small block ad under the name of Jasmine who, the ad said, offered a 'full service with extras' to discerning clients in the comfort of their homes. Jasmine was a busy woman, but there was something in Shelley Jaecks' voice that stopped her hanging up. I'm desperate, she said; I need to make money, I want to know how to set myself up. Eventually Jasmine cut her off mid-sentence (Shelley was explaining the *basic formula* to her) and said, all right, yes, they could meet tomorrow at the shopping centre opposite the school. But how will I know you? asked Shelley. I'll wear something red, said Jasmine.

She did indeed wear red, all the way down to the painted nails. It's like this, said Shelley, once they were seated in the food court: my husband's left me—Men are bastards, said Jasmine—and I've got three boys still at school. He was paying me for a while but then he stopped. I've got debts coming out of my ears. I just want a bit of advice, she said; what to do, what not to do, how to stay safe. Jasmine ran a finger around the rim of her cup. Listen, she said, don't get involved in this unless you really have to. Make him pay child support. It's just to tide me over, said Shelley.

She did the first job in a house in a nearby suburb with Jasmine waiting in the car, then with increasing frequency any number of jobs alone in countless other houses that all felt uncannily the same. She worked in school hours only, and always for cash up front. The streets were quiet, the blinds drawn, the air-conditioners softly hummed. Everything moved slowly, as in a dream.

Meanwhile, with the grey-haired welfare woman's help, she applied for a single-parenting payment and got it. She didn't tell them about her other work. It was not unusual now for her to pick up the kids from school and take them out to dinner. She started buying luxuries for herself too; sometimes after a job she might choose a fifteen- or even twenty-dollar bottle of wine to drink alone in the evening after the children were in bed. As for her battle with her husband, she felt it was a battle she had already won. She didn't need him, or his money—surely that in itself was a victory? He didn't try to see the kids anymore; even he would have to acknowledge that along with his refusal to pay Shelley child support he had relinquished his claim to them.

But then a friend of a mutual friend happened to tell her estranged husband about Shelley's extravagances, how she'd been seen buying new clothes for herself and bottles, not casks, of wine. Her husband reported her—there was little Shelley could say in her defence. It was true, she had undertaken casual work and received undeclared income and in the eyes of the public servants now charged with assessing the information that had been forwarded to them, the ends could not justify the means. She was asked to pay back what she had, officially, been overpaid. But pay it back out of what? she asked. She had put a little money aside against any forthcoming bills but once that was gone she had nothing. How could she pay what she didn't have?

She rang Jasmine for advice; she knew how it would go. You'll need to work more hours, said Jasmine, and do the things you've been refusing. That's where the real money is. Now, when Shelley picked the kids up from school and tried to kiss them, something shivered in her. Sometimes, at night, drunk and just before the pills kicked in, she might have a small moment in which she could see what had happened, how it had happened, and how she might change it. But it was all too complicated, and in the battle between these complications and the numbness to be got from the pills, the pills always won.

It surprised no-one that under these circumstances her husband should seek to drive home the dagger of revenge and apply for custody of the children. He, by contrast, was financially secure and had bought a new house with Belinda in the outer north-east, a rambling old weatherboard with land attached. Here the children could run and play, there was a school nearby, he would reduce his hours in the furniture business and spend more time with his kids who, the court said, Shelley Jaecks was to deliver to him before entering counselling and rehabilitation by the following Friday—today.

With a steak knife she cut herself a length of garden hose, took a bottle of vodka from the freezer and stopped at the local petrol station where she put twenty dollars of petrol in the tank. While inside paying she also bought a big bottle of soft drink and a packet of lollies which she hoped would keep the children happy to the end. When they asked her where they were going she said to Grandma and Grandpa's and, having said this, for some reason Shelley thought it a good idea. Surely now they would help her? She drove the hour there (they lived the other side of Ballarat) but as soon as she saw the empty driveway and the curtains drawn she reversed out again and drove back. This was when she drank most of the vodka. The kids were restless, arguing and demanding something to eat. She stopped and bought three buckets of chips and another bottle of soft drink. She gave them each a tablet and told them to wash it down with the drink (Cooper couldn't swallow his; she had to hide it in a chip) and after a while things went quiet in the back seat, things went quiet throughout the world, aside from the crashing and breaking in poor Shelley Jaecks' head.

She turned off the highway towards home and found a secluded roadside stop out on the old Exford Road. She parked the hatchback under a couple of scraggy acacias, the driver's seat facing the road, then sat and drank for a while. She tried the hose, but the exhaust pipe was double its circumference. After trying to widen the end with a stick and then cutting slits with a pair of nail scissors she still couldn't get it to fit. She got back in the car and drove off to get some tape from the hardware in Sunbury but the car ran out of petrol. The children were still sleeping: she let the windows down a little and locked the doors. It was bright and sunny, early afternoon. She started walking, slipping on the gravel verge, over-correcting and swaying out onto the road. A car veered past and stopped a little way up ahead: a man in overalls got out and looked back. Are you okay? he asked. I've run out of petrol, said Shelley.

Was it the red hatchback? asked the driver. Shelley nodded. There were kids in there, he said. They're asleep, she said. The driver turned and looked at her. You shouldn't leave them there, he said. They're all right, Shelley said, they've got lollies. They were just outside Sunbury. There's a petrol station coming up, said the driver. I need to go to the hardware, said Shelley. The driver didn't argue: he regretted stopping for this woman and wanted to rid himself of her as quickly as he could. She filled up a can at the petrol station and waved the driver on. They pulled up outside the hardware. Without so much as a thank you, Shelley got out and walked inside.

In the bright-lit hardware store she took a roll of fifty-millimetre duct tape from the shelf, shoved it down her jeans and headed for the exit. A security guard was watching and in his windowless office out the back he gestured for her to sit. The duct tape sat on the desk between them, the petrol can on the floor beside Shelley's chair. It was an old routine, he'd been through it many times. You have been observed putting a roll of duct tape down your jeans and attempting to leave the store today without paying: do you deny this? he asked. Shelley shook her head. The guard continued: Do you have an explanation as to why you have attempted to take this item from the store today without paying? Shelley looked up at him, tried to keep her head still and her eyes focussed. My husband sent me down here to buy it, she said, but he doesn't know that I've spent all the housekeeping money on grog. If he finds out he will bash me, he bashes me all the time: I just need to get through today then sort things out but if I don't come home in the meantime with his tape he'll kill me. And the petrol? asked the guard. But now Shelley's head had flopped down on her chest again.

It was uncountable, the number of times the security guard had heard something like this, every day there was another story, but he decided that today with this woman he would salve his conscience for never having believed any of them. Without blinking he took out his wallet, drew from it a ten-dollar note and handed it across the table to her. Here, he said, buy the tape, and don't come back here again. Shelley picked up the note, the tape and the petrol, and went out into the store to pay.

It was only an hour's walk back to the car. The children were still sleeping. She put the petrol in the tank, then set to work on the hose, fitting the splayed end as best she could against the butt end of the exhaust pipe and winding a good length of duct tape around both. She stepped back, pleased. She ran the hose end through a gap in one of the rear windows and taped up tightly around it. She wound all the other windows up and ran a line of tape along the joins, just to be sure. She got back into the front seat and took a last swig from the vodka bottle.

When she turned the key in the ignition two things happened. The first was that the hose blew off the exhaust pipe again with a loud pop; the second, almost simultaneously, was that the three children woke with a start and said *Mum?* Just a minute, said Shelley Jaecks. She got out, went back around to the rear of the car and with more tape tried to attach the hose again. She got back in. Where are we? asked Thomas. What's the hose doing here? asked Jake. Shh, she said. She turned the ignition again; again the hose popped off. At the fifth attempt, something in

Shelley snapped. She ripped the hose from the window and hurled it into the adjoining paddock, scaring up a flock of cockatoos that had just settled there to peck for seed.

Over the years many people have loudly wondered why I started this donkey business, what made me do it, why I deigned to bend down low to help my fellow humans and set them upon my ass. It was not as if anyone told me to. On the contrary, it was in direct defiance of my superiors' orders that I looked deep inside myself that day and found the part that didn't want to kill or be killed but live and let live. I wasn't the first or even the finest but once dead I became their symbol. They needed me. They called what I did *mateship*, as if it really were a *ship*, some great vessel that would carry us all out of this quagmire into some glorious imagined future, a hulk full this time not of humanity's detritus but its best. I became an ethos, an affirmation. We are all, every one of us, men with donkeys, and at the drop of a hat we will throw all we own aside to bend down low and lift our injured up. We're good people, we care for our neighbours, we'll always go out of our way to help.

What is compassion? What is it for? Why do we

bother? Why be selfless when you can be selfish, humble when you could be haughty? Is it that we see selflessness as a selfish thing? That the greatest danger in stopping to help is that someone might think you're putting on airs? Maybe those passing by on the other side think helping an act of self-aggrandisement, not of mercy? Perhaps we are more concerned with seeming than with being? Or is it that we just don't have the time, that we are too busy hurrying from one place to the next? When we see that person lying on the side of the road—attacked by thieves, usurers' henchmen, the daggers of self-doubt, the annihilating impulse—aren't we just worried about the *complications*? The business of caring is complicated, few would willingly do it. Is this why the Priest and the Levite pass by?

When Lasseter gave me his map and set me and my donkey on the way to the Inland Sea I felt like I finally had some teleology to be going on with. With its waters I would heal all, not just the ragged few; I would not be compelled all the time to turn around and help this or that person out. I'd not have to hear all these stories that were quite frankly often very distressing to me. I could push on and tell all these troubled souls that I'd be back one day soon with cures aplenty. But it didn't work out like that. I could not pass them by. A moan, a wail, a whimper, and I was there like a dog to a bone.

Shelley dried her tears. I think the hose you use is the one you see on washing machines, I said. But where do you get it? she said. I don't know, I said, perhaps direct from the manufacturer? It still should have worked, she said. True, I said. There was a pause. Well, I said, let's leave all that for now: there is little to be gained from this talk of hoses. For the first time Shelley smiled.

I worked on her all afternoon. Difficult case! Resourceful Simpson! Cunning, creative, resourceful Simpson! While the children frolicked out on the paddock, back and forth I went to my pannier bags, mixing this with that, applying one thing externally, offering another internally, bringing what colour I could to her cheeks. I lay down my poultices, brought the filth to the surface. I drew out the poison, bled her of bad blood, gave calm to her confusion. I put the last of the bandages on and led a battle-weary Shelley Jaecks to the fence. Her kids were still running around out there in that beautiful late-afternoon light. Come and have a go, Mum! they shouted. Shelley let herself through the gate.

They played until the light was nearly gone; Shelley riding Murphy, the children, full of lollies and Fanta, dancing around her like dryads. Eventually I whistled him up, and, either energised by all this fun and games or desperate to escape it, he pricked up his ears and trotted towards me. The boys had made him a garland of Paterson's curse; he arrived at the fence and put his head over. Leave the hatchback here, I said to Shelley, and come ride upon my ass. I slung the pannier bags over my shoulder. Gee-up, I said, and Murphy walked. The children followed. The rain was still an hour away; the breeze had hardly stirred. We encountered no-one on the way.

Half an hour's leisurely journey and we were outside Shelley's plain brick house in Melton. A bike was still in the drive. I helped her down. She asked would I stay, showed me the garage, offered provender for me and my beast. Alas, no, I cannot stay, I said; I am on my way to the Inland Sea and I have a long journey ahead. Shelley Jaecks thanked me with a few kind words and ruffled the hair of her brood.

So what will happen now? Distant from me, and hard to say. She's been restored, and will survive. She'll go inside, clean up the mess. Ask for mediation, go for shared custody if she can. The scars will heal, eventually. Perhaps they will pick up from where they left off? And perhaps not. The truth is it was no longer any concern of mine; I'd bandaged her wounds, brought her down through hellfire to the beach. That was the best I could do, all I could do, for all our injured, until that far-off day when I will stand knee-deep in the healing water baptising all our downtrodden in it.

3

AN UNFORTUNATE LIFE

The heavens opened. This was the rain of which I have previously spoken, and under its relentless assault we decamped to a hayshed off the Toolern Vale road. Murphy was not well. I made up a decoction of wild fennel and horehound and gave it to him two-hourly. We stayed there a week drying out. In that time I got to thinking, of how this trip might be our last and how I might set things down against my inevitable demise. I will tell of the country I have travelled through, I thought, the patients I have met, the afflictions I have seen, the stories I have heard, so that future generations might one day stand my story up against the sanctioned ones and see where their sympathies lie. I will not be afraid to speak for the people,

I said, who were not afraid of me.

At last the rain cleared to showers, though Murphy was little improved. I gave him a poke and spoke in his ear: Come, my friend, let us tarry no more. He did not blink, his ears did not twitch, his demeanour did not change, but soon enough he was shuffling forward, the same old steady gait, ready for come what may.

We lunched at the Coimadai monument on a can of creamed corn a supplicant had left, then descended the winding road down to the perilous Lerderderg Gorge. We wheeled west, and began following the treed gullies of the Lerderderg's tributaries deep into the Blackwood Ranges. None of this was easy going—the gullies were still wet, Murphy was still wheezing—but experience had told me (twenty-eight attempts!) that once through this wooded green we would come out to the flat ground that would take us all the way to the Interior. After some days we emerged from the Blackwood Ranges just west of Spargo Creek, the bush now broken by pine plantations and clear-felled paddocks of dirt and shattered wood. We rested at a roadside stop, I gave Murphy some more of his decoction, then we pushed on. But we had not gone very far when we came across a one-legged man standing on a goat. Around the man's neck was a rope, tied to the branch above. The goat was newly shorn. For God's sake, Denis, what are you doing? I said. The goat won't move, said Denis Wrycroft. But can't you get down? I asked. Denis shook his head. I led Murphy alongside: although it was clearly an unwelcome marriage the goat was good enough not to move. Stand on my donkey, I said. He did. But what do I do now? he said. I'm thinking, I said. What about I get off the donkey and stand back on the goat, said Denis; then you get up on the donkey and undo the noose? I could not see his logic. Why don't you just undo the noose yourself, from there? I said. I might fall, said Denis. But wasn't this your intention? I said. Get my stick, he said. Where is it? I asked. It's in the grass. I retrieved the stick. Now you hold one end of the stick, he said, and I'll hold the other for safety and with my free hand I'll undo the noose. This he managed to do. Now try to sit, I said. I can't, he said. Why not? I said. Because of the leg, he said. I was not sure exactly in what way this prevented him sitting but he was adamant about it. Why don't you lie down, then, I said, half across the donkey and half across the goat, then slide down backwards till you touch the ground? Denis Wrycroft accomplished this with ease. Can you walk? I asked. He shook his head.

It was in his one remaining leg that Denis Wrycroft had the gout, the other had been taken from him in the war. Walking therefore was never an easy thing, despite the government-subsidised prosthesis he had spent so long mastering. I lashed him stretcher-style to Murphy's flank and handed him his stick. I put a rope on the goat. You're going from bad to worse, I said. Denis Wrycroft gave me a wincing smile. From worse to appalling, he said.

Denis Wrycroft was twenty-nine and a half years old when he volunteered to fight in the war that followed the war that followed the war that followed the war to end all wars and was now cultivating the daisies he would soon be pushing up. He lived on a farm near the hamlet of Barkstead, to where I now relayed him. In its day his weatherboard cottage stood among the greenery of a well-watered paddock in the shade of two newly planted pines. But that was in its day. Time had spread that green paddock with weeds and broken the backs of the two old pines. Like most who saw me he was well disposed towards me. His so-called daughter, however, was not. A curmudgeonly woman, she could not tolerate the idea of me, much less my demonstrable presence in 'her' house.

She drove a little blue Hyundai, and I was always very careful, on approaching, to check that the car in question was not parked in the drive.

Denis kept chickens, and always slaughtered a bird in my honour. I stood and watched for a long time as my still-drunk one-legged gout-ridden sexagenarian chased (if that is the word) his chosen chook around the pen. It was a scrawny thing he then held up, mangy, diseased-looking, flapping feebly, with little in the way of feathers left to pluck. After we had eaten it, with roast potatoes and home-grown beans, the table was cleared and I set out the stones. I had picked them up from a building site in Burnley. They gave us a précis of Denis's present state of health and of the cures we might use. The three blue metals I arranged into a triangle, a stone at each corner, and into the centre of this triangle I put the piece of concrete. Denis put his finger on it. But before he told me his troubles and how precisely his life of late had gone from worse to appalling he felt it first necessary to repeat his *entire* story, in all its intricate detail, so I should be up with the facts.

Denis Wrycroft had returned from the war that followed the war that followed the war that followed the war to end all wars soon after he'd left for it, having lost his leg to a landmine five days after landing. But getting out again so quickly was a happy turn of events, given that only two days before embarking something very memorable had occurred, something that meant that for the duration of the trip, the landing and the few days bivouacking that followed, Denis's thoughts were entirely elsewhere. This 'elsewhere', specifically, was the local General Store, and more specifically its front counter, and the orange curtain that hung across the door behind it, dividing the shop from the house out the back. It was through this curtain and at this counter that the vision of Mary Rose Stafford had first appeared.

Six years younger than Denis but years older than him in many other important respects, Mary Rose Stafford was a vision of womanhood. He was not the only man to open the General Store door and hear the bell jingle and look to the orange curtain with a butterfly in his heart. Mary Rose Stafford was tall, shapely, with breasts, it seemed to Denis, that had just the right proportionate relationship to her hips, as her waist did, in its way, to her neck and ankles, so that the whole thing, again, to Denis's eyes, appeared to have achieved some mystical

Golden Mean. Her face was pretty, too, but not in any sort of dainty daisy-chain way: no, Mary Rose's beauty was of a much more ethereal kind. Even the faint brown freckles on her nose could not diminish it. Her eyes were hazel, rimmed by dark lashes, and her long hair mousy brown. She wore short skirts, and blouses with necklines that while nowhere near allowing a clue to her cleavage gave glimpses of the shallow ditches above her collarbone and the alabaster field of her upper chest.

Did I mention that Denis Wrycroft, by contrast, was as ugly as a hatful of arseholes? Of course this shouldn't matter, but naturally it did. He'd fallen out of a tree at the age of three and a half and had his nose flattened back level with his cheekbones. He had very bad skin, few teeth and enormous muttonchop sideburns. He tried to avoid mirrors wherever he could, but alas almost everything was a mirror, reflecting his ugliness back at him, not least the fact of Mary Rose's beauty. Denis Wrycroft never knew his father, and his mother only for the time it took him to be weaned; from then on parental responsibilities fell to the state, and after that to the charitable arm of the Christian church. For Denis the main disadvantage of being raised by Christian men, aside from the obvious risks, was that they never told him he was ugly. His mother, he was sure, would not have held back—that's what mothers are for—but the do-gooders felt bound to do good, which in his case was to chuck him under the chin with a crooked finger and tell him what a good-looking young fella he was. This lie he believed for many years—his adoptive parents adopted it too—and it was in the spirit of it that on getting his orders to go to war he asked Mary Rose Stafford to marry him.

To Denis Wrycroft it was all perfectly natural; there was hardly a soldier who went off to fight without first putting an innocent woman in this awkward situation. So it was equally natural to him that Mary Rose Stafford, whom he had said no more than a dozen words to in the half a dozen times they'd met, had answered yes. Yes. She smiled in a way that Denis found difficult to interpret, gave him his change and slipped back through the orange curtain. Denis kept the penny she'd given him as a memento, confident it would be the coin to stop the bullet that would otherwise take his life, and prepared to ship out to South-East Asia, sure in the knowledge his love would be waiting for him when he returned.

It is debatable whether the loss of the leg made

Denis's physical appearance any worse than it already was, given the extent of his ugliness, but he could find no other explanation for his fiancée's coolness towards him when he came back with one leg less than the two he had gone with in the summer of '66. But didn't he realise, she said, that she was joking, that she couldn't have been serious, that she'd said yes just to humour him, that she was already engaged at the time—here she turned and called out through the curtain—and that she was now married, to John. John was standing in the doorway. Who on earth is this? he said. It's just a local fella, said Mary Rose. By Christ you're ugly, said her husband. Don't say that, John, said Mary Rose, there's nothing he can do.

So, contradicting his original intentions, Denis Wrycroft returned from the war not to Mary Rose's bed and bosom, as he'd hoped, but to the potato farm of his adoptive parents and had the opportunity to grieve neither the loss of his bride nor his leg before his adoptive father had him up on the tractor spraying the paddocks. This is the time of plenty, said his adoptive father: sow and we shall reap. And sow and reap they did. Denis barely had time to draw breath. In the whirring cycle of sowing and reaping that followed, through the late '60s and into the '70s, he hardly noticed first his adoptive father then his adoptive mother pass away, or the haste with which his hasty marriage to a local girl called Dawn disintegrated or when exactly she took off with the mechanic from Creswick, the real father, he later realised, of the daughter born four months *post matrimonium*. Nor, in pursuing the prosperity that service to his country would surely bring, did he see the topsoil of the farm being washed away, notice the trees dropping their branches, smell the stink of the bore water, or register when exactly it was that superphosphate salesmen became landcare consultants. The farm had gone to the dogs—the paddocks cracked, the weeds unsprayed, the potatoes all gone to seed. He applied for an invalid pension and got it: he had eczema, high blood pressure, pancreatitis; the gout in his one good leg often left him chair-ridden for days. This man whose life had always been circumscribed by a circle of loneliness was now utterly, irretrievably, alone.

In an effort to relieve some of this loneliness, Denis now hobbled off every morning into the nearby town to drink at the pub and bet on the horses. He became a familiar sight between there and home and each time he collapsed by the side of the road the local police would pick him up, lecture him and drive him home. But the next day he was at it again. He became increasingly dishevelled, and increasingly a victim of bad health. He was now carrying a goitre in his neck the size of a grapefruit. The next time he collapsed, out on the Korweinguboora road, the police chose to take him not home but to the emergency department of the nearest hospital where, a few days later, the long-lost so-called daughter decided to re-enter his life—just as, conveniently, Denis looked about to depart it. She had come to 'put his affairs in order', she said, as she stood beside her so-called father's bed, which was another way of saying she'd come to pack him off to the Golden Years Private Nursing Home, inherit the 'family' farm and build her dream home on it. Here, with her cats and knick-knacks, Robin would live out a leisured retirement, the remainder of the property being sold off to fund it after her so-called father's demise, surely only a few months away.

But Denis Wrycroft was no fool, it was just that life had a habit of making him look like one. After he had celebrated his sixty-sixth birthday with a simple cake-and-candle ceremony in the games room at Golden Years, Denis discharged himself, moved back to the farm and bought a small flock of angora goats that he penned in the paddock nearest the house. The daughter thought his mind was failing, which gave her good reason to hope soon his heart would too. But Denis's goats were part of a wider plan to which only I, Jack Simpson, was privy, and this plan was to do in his twilight years what he had wanted to do for the previous thirty-seven, and that was to woo and marry the widow Mary Rose Pate, née Stafford, the vision of whose transcendent beauty had not left him since his eyes had caught it and his heart recorded it all those years ago.

Now as for Mary Rose Pate's husband, John, the man behind the orange curtain, he had confidently thought he could avoid the messy side of that very messy war by pleading his skill as a bookkeeper, a job he held at the Victoria Barracks until late 1967 when, while crossing St Kilda Road one day, he got hit by a tram. From afar the one-legged flat-faced Denis Wrycroft watched Mary Rose Pate née Stafford mourn her loss, return to the shop with her parents, run it alone after their passing and, upon its sale to the city couple who would turn it into a tearooms, move to a rundown miner's cottage near Barkstead. She painted it a bold yellow and blue, ran a banksia rose over the trellis at the gate, and began to make a modest living selling blueberry jam and hand-knitted angora jumpers at the local Sunday markets. One of her main suppliers for the wool needed to knit these jumpers had, as it turned out, for the past few years been the farmer Denis Wrycroft, the ugly twenty-nine-year-old she still remembered (not without a certain affection) from the mid-1960s. Mary Rose Pate liked to shear Denis's goats herself, to attain, as she said, the best-quality fibre, and this is why Denis Wrycroft had taken the whole goat to her house that day and not just its already-shorn fleece.

With a goat on a rope in one hand and his walking stick in the other, he arrived at Mary Rose Pate's house around noon. The sun was on her back verandah; her new black labrador puppy flipped and flopped around their feet. At sixty years of age her beauty was if anything more radiant to Denis's eyes than it had been all those years before. Mary Rose Pate sheared the goat, with long sensual sweeps of her arm, and bundled the fleece to her breast. She paid him for it and suggested they have a drink, to celebrate the transaction. She opened a cheap bottle of wine—and that was where the trouble started.

They talked of Life, its forking paths, and how one

leads to another but never to the one you hoped for. They talked of many things. It was not until they'd finished the second bottle that Denis finally put the rope on the goat. They were both a little drunk. Thank you for the conversation, said Denis, sadly. Mary Rose smiled, and gently touched his arm. This was Denis's cue (as he saw it) to pull her violently towards him, kiss her on the lips and bury his tongue in her mouth. Mary Rose Pate didn't know what to do. Forget the past, said Denis passionately, still clutching her to him, come and live with me and be my companion till death. Mary Rose Pate peeled him off her. Thank you for your offer, she said, but I'm not sure that I can. Denis looked at her with moist eyes, sighed, then turned away. Ah, Life! Mary Rose Pate watched him go—he was not a bad man, he was just so impossibly ugly.

Denis made his way homeward—a long journey for a man in his condition. He walked the gravel verge of Barkstead Road, opened a gate, cut across some paddocks, then turned down a back road towards home. A little way along he tethered the goat to a road post, and sat down with the aid of his stick. He spent a long while like that, thinking. He got to his feet, and, in a complicated series of manoeuvres, set the goat under the branch of a nearby tree, took off its rope bridle and rein, climbed aboard, and, with the aid of his stick, stood up on its back. He threw one end of the rope over the branch and made a noose with the other. He put the noose around his neck and whacked the goat with the stick. But the goat wouldn't move. He whacked it again. This was a goat that would have put a donkey to shame. In the end he whacked it so hard that the stick flew from his hand and landed in the grass.

It was a complicated business, the stones, the ritual, the diagnosis. We did not finish until well after midnight and by this time Denis's other goats were poking their heads in through the kitchen window, asking to be fed. Throughout it all Denis sat glumly, his moist eyes gazing at the pattern of stones on the table, listening to my droning monody. I will not give a full catalogue of his ailments here, it would take me the better part of a week, but besides them the man had a broken heart and what cure was there for that? With a jerry can of water from the Inland Sea anything was possible but that was still a long way ahead of me yet. All I could do in the meantime (all I have ever really done) to alleviate the blights upon the bodies of their victims left by those spiteful diseases Fate and Time was to administer my poultices and potions, my incantatory fictions, my sideshow bombast and quackery as best I could. And this I did, to Denis Wrycroft's satisfaction, from the serving of dinner and on into the night. Is that better, Denis? I asked. A little, yes, Denis said.

The next morning I boiled great bunches of Scotch broom, gorse and stinging nettle that I gathered from out on the paddocks and over the following two hours decanted from this a small quantity of essential oil that I then administered by spoon homoeopathically to the patient. I held his head back to get it down. We must have looked like two old monkeys picking their nits. I then listened for a while with my homemade stethoscope to the interior of his skull. Little was stirring there. A bit of shellfire, otherwise all silent. I put on the poultice of mud and blood and called Murphy to the door. It is a ritual we have been through many times and Murphy knows it by heart. I put a bandage around old Denis's head and hoist him onto Murphy's back. Like a well-trained pony at a children's fête Murphy does without bidding his business. Me holding the slack rein and walking beside we take old Denis on a tour of his battlefields, up the main track from the house, along the north-eastern fence line, around the far northern boundary, past the empty dam, the windmill and the trough, then back along the main track home.

By the time we have completed the tour, the mud and blood have seeped out through Denis's poultice into the bandage and begun to run down his face and he is back in the paddy fields and the shellfire with Mary Rose's penny in his pocket again. At the back verandah he dismounts Murphy with a spring in his step that he has not felt for years. He looks almost handsome. He turns around, I turn around (let the whole world turn around!) and we both look back at the paddocks through which we have walked. There are many who disbelieve my miracles; there are the faithful few who do not. It's up to you. All across Denis Wrycroft's useless paddocks a verdant carpet rolled.

Back inside, I had barely begun the next part of my voodoo when I heard the Hyundai in the drive. Murphy was still tethered to the back verandah post. I could hear the so-called daughter's footsteps on the gravel and the screeching sound of her voice. Soon there would be trouble. I've been with Jack Simpson, he will say. Shut up, she will say; there is no such person, it's just voices in your head. And how do I know, Denis will counter, that you're not just a voice in my head?

I untied Murphy. In my flickering black-and-white cowboy dreams I have sometimes got him up to a gallop. From down in the gully, behind a stand of trees, I could see the so-called daughter on the back verandah, scanning the paddocks for a sighting. I quietly cluck-clucked Murphy forward, and watched her turn back inside.

4

THE JOLLYLESS REFUGEE

The weather had cleared, the going was easy. The clip-clop of hooves on bitumen is a crisp, invigorating thing. I was on the back roads again, as far away as I could be from people and their problems, skirting around the back of Creswick, the Tullaroop Creek gully on my right. Of the scenery there was little to report: the same receding road, pasture paddocks, some cows, fewer trees. I hoped to reach the town of Lexton before evening fell on what was now my thirteenth day. I knew a park there, a rotunda, a picnic table and a tree, my perquisites buried beneath.

Though the weather had cleared, Murphy's pulmonary problems had not: he still struggled for breath, still had that glassy look in his eye, and would sometimes disconcertingly stop without warning in the middle of the road to rest. There was no point me trying to goad him along; he would not move until he was ready. I just had to stand there and take in the scenery, watch a cow jawing its cud or a falcon on a wimpling wing. It was all peace and quiet out there when the clip-clop stopped—I might have been the only human left on earth. Sometimes I think I am, and that all these others are mere simulacra of what a human could be. But *what is a human*? Don't ask a donkey. Of all the questions you may ask your ass—Did I say you could stop? Are you looking at me? Could you go a little faster, please?—this is one you should refrain from asking. They have no aptitude for metaphysics. By a campfire one night, brandy-drunk and in a profound state of existential crisis (I lived and yet did not live; was flesh and yet not), I put this question to my special companion. His response was not to give me doe eyes or a monologue from Kant, but to drop his member from its sheath and piss a great puddle on the ground.

I have not bothered him with such questions since—but such questions still bother me. *What is a human?* What are they for? I have spent my life, my first and second, fixing them up, getting them out of trouble, but

I am no closer to understanding. Do they have a higher purpose, other than the one of asking? And these lumpen proles, these 'battlers' I keep bumping into, what are they here for and do I care? Was I really the holy ministrant back there in Shrapnel Gully, as accounts of me later would have it, or was I just putting on airs? Who was I helping, the wounded in body, or me, the wounded in soul?

It was a hellish, horrible place. But what made it most hellish was the knowledge that we were playthings, and while we ducked the singing shrapnel and looked for a toehold in the mud our leaders were pushing miniature versions of us around a big table in their ships offshore. Has anything changed? Are those bumbling aristocrats any different from today's elected aloof? Planning campaigns in a headquarters far removed, issuing orders for more cannon fodder, collecting data on the wounded and tendering for advisors to interpret the figures. But that's not the worst of it. This new generation of soft-skinned generals have turned their forebears' follies to their own marketing ends. *We've become the symbol of the nation!* Thrown to our deaths by indifferent men, our courage and laughter in the face of adversity now sells their snake oil for them. It gives some backbone to their spineless, snivelling, jellyfish souls.

Technically I was a deserter back there in the Hellespont; I should have been blindfolded and shot. I did what I wanted, I was hoeing my own row. When your bosses are a bunch of brainless buffoons, what else can you do? I spotted Murphy and put a bandage bridle on him: no-one told me I had to. I went up the gully and brought a wounded man down: that was my idea. The Indians called me Bahadur, Bravest of the Brave; they wept when I took my predestined bullet and put wildflowers on my grave. I talked to them many times, in their camp at the foot of the gully where they liveried their mules. They spoke to me of their ancient teachings, of the man who went to the Palace of Death and the things he was told there. They instructed me in self-knowledge, gained by stern reflection and selfless acts of social duty. They told me of their hierophants, and of how my soul was a thumb-sized thing that would transmigrate elsewhere later. But above all my Hindu teachers made me see the transience of this fleshly existence and the possibilities of a life beyond. (How strange, then, Lasseter's vial.) The Indians would have burned my body, if they could, but fighting was bad that day. I lay out on the track, my ghost hovering above. While no-one was looking I sneaked back in. They say the soul not ushered to Paradise is destined ever after to be errant; it wanders the countryside, blabbering. So it was.

Night was falling over Lexton as we made our way to the park in the centre of town. The council hadn't mown the grass for a while; Murphy started mowing it for them. I tied him to the picnic table, took off the pannier bags and dropped them under the pine. They are ubiquitous. Grown from seeds souvenired from the one that once stood above the happy hunting grounds of Gallipoli, cultivated in returned servicemen's greenhouses the length and breadth of the land, ceremoniously planted in parks and reserves, their seeds scattered by cockatoo shit and the wind, in many parts of the country *Pinus halepensis* is a weed. This one was planted in 1968, the year the Lexton Tigers won the flag by a kick. I always sought them out, these pines, whenever I needed to sit and think, like Buddha under his Bo Tree. After making camp I untied my entrenching tool and dug up my store to see what I'd left. In the Lexton hole I had buried—twenty, thirty years ago?—a bottle of brandy, two ampoules of morphine, a pair of socks, a note to myself (*Be patient*) and a book. It was *The Lucky Country* by Donald Horne, in a Penguin paperback edition. My dog-ear was still in it. The night air was coming down; I threw a blanket over Murphy and an extra layer of clothing on myself. I snapped an ampoule, uncapped the bottle and by the light of the little penlight torch that a manic-depressive retail assistant from Ardeer once gave me I read the book and drank the brandy until the gentle hand of Morpheus led me through the Gates of Sleep.

It took me a while to realise where I was, where I was going, indeed, what I'd become. I was an ass: dull, clumsy, ignorant. On my back I carried the whole nation and every sickness in it; every canker of the heart, every affliction of the soul, every mortal wound. This nation, strangely enough, looked like it had been cut from plywood, though it was much heavier to carry. You could see the Gulf and the Bight, the spear of the Cape and the long sweeping line of the west; the capital cities, moderately spaced. Over this map the blighted teemed, mostly around the growth areas of the coastal fringe, like ants on a picnic table. Had there been an observer to observe these things, no doubt I would have looked like one of those clowns in the circus, when on top of a broomstick they balance a ball, and on top of that ball a table, and on top of that table a lawn mower, with a birdcage on top of that. Indeed, the cut-out island continent with all its people was not all I, the ass, had to carry, for balanced atop that were its mightiest hopes, deepest anxieties, most poignant delusions. On top of this I somehow managed to keep from slipping the egalitarian ideal. On top of that tolerance, fairness. And then, most extraordinarily of all, on top of all that, I had to balance a statue of Murphy and myself, cast in bronze, our cargo a stiff-legged soldier hanging on for dear life. I also had the sensation, in this dream, that I had been travelling for a long time, though in the context of world history not that long, and that I still had a long way to go. The path up to now had been reliably straight and relatively unrocky, which was lucky, given my burden, and throughout the course of my journey the sky was always blue. I never slept, as such, but my waking was a kind of sleeping: every moment I spent in a somnolent state, like a koala full of leaves. Perhaps, I thought, it was this happy, half-sleeping state that allowed me to carry my monstrous burden and yet not feel any pain?

In the dream I was just thinking this, how my burden

seemed excessive, how tranquillised I felt, when in the middle of the road there appeared two haystacks, identical in every way. (Asses must go through this sort of thing all the time.) Though while stationary I felt even more keenly my burden and though my weariness and hunger were great, I determined to stop before these two haystacks and examine them carefully for any differences. There were none, so far as I could see. They were the same width, the same height, the same depth, and therefore presumably the same volume. The aroma coming off them both smelled, to my ass's nose, the same. There were as many steps to one as to the other. I could not decide between them. Just as I was about to cast my vote for the stack on the right, I saw something in the stack on the left; just as I was about to decide on the stack on the left, I found the same thing hidden in the stack on the right. Obviously I would have to eat from one of these stacks—I was very hungry, my burden was heavy, there was a long way to go—but which one was it going to be?

Every time the sun dropped towards the western horizon another sun rose in the east. This was repeated, again and again, with only a momentary shadowing of the sky to distinguish the passage of time. Weeks passed, then months, and still I stood before the stacks. I was starving, but at the same time strangely sated. Standing before the haystacks knowing I could eat whichever one I chose, anytime I liked, right down to the ground, gave me enormous inner satisfaction. What reason was there to move? Years passed, and still I stood there. The haystacks didn't change, they still looked and smelled as fresh and inviting as before. I faded away, faded away almost to nothing, I was a mere shadow of the ass I had once been. Then a traveller came down the road—I'd not seen anyone for years. Well, here's a sight, he said: two lovely haystacks, big and fresh and waiting to be eaten; and here an ass, standing before them. Tell me, ass, he said, why don't you eat your fill? I turned my skinny neck towards him. But I am, I said, in my way.

I woke to Murphy braying. The light in the nearby toilet block flickered, the bottle of brandy lay empty beside me and through the branches of the Lexton Lone Pine I could see a black sky full of stars. Murphy brayed again and nodded his mule head. Now I saw: there was a man sitting huddled on a bench in the rotunda, shivering, moaning. He hadn't seen me, sitting as I was cross-legged like a yogi contemplating the haystacks on my way down the eightfold path. He had brown skin, a rough beard and a Brisbane Lions beanie. He didn't look well. Around his neck on a piece of string was a cardboard sign: *PLase Help*. I approached, and asked how long he'd been there. Three weeks, said the man, in an unfamiliar accent. Curious. And what is your story? I asked, fully aware of what I was letting myself in for. You will listen? said the man, looking up at me, surprised. That's what I do, I said. My name is Jack Simpson, and that there is my donkey, Murphy. We made our names in the Great War, at Gallipoli, against the Turks. The country needed a martyr. Now I crisscross the countryside, doing good. I can afford to tarry awhile and listen to your tale: truth be told, I've just had a mighty good sleep. Who are you, I said, where do you come from, and in a land of fatted calves why do you look so horribly thin?

His name was Javed. He had just walked from the Murray via Wycheproof to a vineyard outside Avoca—but there was no work for him there. For the past two and a half years he had followed the seasonal trail, Mildura to Robinvale, over the border to Tooleybuc, back again and down through Wood Wood, Nyah and Swan Hill, and in the late season south to the vineyards of the Victorian Pyrenees. This was pretty much the way it had been since they let him out of the camp. He'd hacked meat, picked fruit, driven taxis and sent what he could back home. He had travelled and worked alongside his countrymen, including some he had shared the boat with, but then he had grown restless and for some time now had been travelling alone. His only real emotional tie was to the wife and three young children he had left behind. They were safe now, in a camp over the border, but he had not seen them since he left, nearly seven years ago.

No sooner had Javed mentioned his wife and children than he was blubbering into what I could see was a very dirty handkerchief. In fact, the closer I looked, the more I saw how truly filthy he was. His trousers were stained at the knees and cuffs with rich red Sunraysia soil; he had dirt under his fingernails and in the weathered cracks of his skin; his beard was unwashed and matted; one of his shoes was laced with twine. I offered him a clean rag, the one I use for polishing my buttons, and let him hoot and snort until he was breathing through his nose again. He took an untouched corner and dabbed his eyes. I have come to the end, he said: my journey is finished. I looked around us. What sort of place was this to finish a journey? I made up a tincture to put on his tongue. He was entirely trusting. Well if, as you say, this is the end, I said, then tell me, what was the beginning?

One hundred years of suffering had brought Javed to this place—his people had always been persecuted but more violently of late. He sought out an agent called Masooma, well known in their district, and paid him thirteen thousand Australian dollars in borrowed money to get him to the country many had spoken of as paradise. There, they said, he would find a job, save money, bring his wife and children out and start a new life.

In the middle of the night along with half a dozen other desperate men he was loaded into the back of a truck and driven to the capital, where, at the end of a quiet street, they were transferred to a minibus. It was covered in dust and had obviously been travelling roads far from the capital. Quickly, quietly, false passports in their hands, they made their way across the border. That night they slept on mats on the living-room floor of a man called Salim and after breakfast they boarded a bus that took them across mountains and through deep valleys to a port city in the south. They arrived there in the evening, hungry and tired, and were driven to the airport. There, said Javed, in his broken English, mingled with the smell of engine fumes and sweat, was the unmistakable and to him wholly new smell of the sea.

They flew all night, Javed half-dozing and looking out the window at the lights of the subcontinent below. The eastern horizon was lightening when they banked and began their descent. He looked around at the others and saw in them all the same anticipation and dread. At the airport they had been told to look for a man called Mr Puntodewo, and indeed, they had no sooner come off the travelator than a short man in a pink polo shirt with a cardboard sign saying *Mr Puntodewo* appeared. He led them to a side door where two policemen stood guard; Mr Puntodewo nodded and the door was pushed open for him. He led the group down a corridor, then another, then briefly out onto the tarmac and back in through another door. Now they were in the baggage-claim area. They collected their bags and followed Mr Puntodewo out into the heavy tropical air, then down a ramp into a car park where a new minibus was waiting.

Around lunchtime they arrived in a small village in

the hinterland behind the sea and took a long winding driveway edged with tall palms up to a house high on stilts. This was Mr Hussein's place, and one by one the men in the minibus were introduced to him. Mr Hussein was always smiling; Javed was not sure if this was a good thing or not. He told them they would be staying at his house for a while, that they would like it in Australia, that they would be there soon, that within a month they would have their permits and after three months their passports, that the Australian government was a kind and considerate one which would give them ten thousand dollars each in cash to start a new life there. Mr Hussein then held up a photograph of a big white cruise ship on a big blue ocean. Your ship, very soon, he said.

Mr Puntodewo drove away and the visitors were taken from the main house to a big barn-like structure with its own bathroom and toilet and a small balcony from where you could glimpse the ocean through the trees. They were well fed, three meals a day, and when it was not raining, which it often was, they would spend their daylight hours wandering in the lush tropical garden and at night would lie under mosquito nets writing letters by lamplight home. There were others like themselves, in other huts dotted around the property, and every other day more people arrived.

By the end of the third week, the huts on Mr Hussein's villa were full to overflowing; Javed estimated there would have been at least three hundred people. Rumour came to him that this was the quota and then, soon after that, eight big buses appeared, snaking up Mr Hussein's driveway. Everyone was loaded in. There was no air-conditioning, the hot rain pelted down; they left the main road and wended their way down to a tiny fishing village on the far western side of the island. Javed could see the beach, and some fishing boats moored offshore. The buses stopped, the drivers got out and started talking to a man who kept pointing out to sea. Presumably they were waiting for the white ship to appear. It was very stuffy in the bus now that it had stopped, and everyone was desperate to get outside. But the driver had locked the doors. The sky darkened, there was still no white ship. All the drivers were sitting on the sand at the water's edge, smoking and talking, looking out at the darkening sea. A half-moon rose and hung above the water. They must have waited a couple of hours, said Javed, while the beach slowly widened, until it was all beach, way out, and the last fishing boat was resting on the sand. The man who had spoken to the drivers earlier walked out across the sand flats. He wore white trousers and in the dull moonlight you could see him pushing here and there with his foot. He turned and waved a white handkerchief back towards the shore.

Then it was all action. The bus doors opened and everyone got out. The driver went round the back and started unloading the bags—they were allowed one small bag only, barely enough to keep a change of clothes in—and then, from a box in the luggage compartment they were each given a bottle of water and a biscuit. This, apparently, was all they needed, and it was precisely this gesture, Javed recalled, above all other things, that convinced him their dash to freedom would be over in a matter of hours. By now the man out on the sand had rolled his trousers up and was waving the white handkerchief even more vigorously, indicating they should follow. Three other crew members had joined him out there now, one with a rope slung over his shoulder. As a mass, everyone rolled up their own trousers and skirts and set out across the wet sand.

Javed could still not see the ship. He kept his eyes on the person in front of him, or on his own feet. He could hear the buses whining their way back up the hill. Crabs scurried sideways, in the puddles and pools small fish shook themselves out of the sand. They weren't walking long before the person in front of him stopped. It took Javed a while to realise what was going on. The captain and his three crew were climbing aboard one of the fishing boats, an old, rickety-looking thing, more a toy boat held together with tape and string than a vessel built to take three hundred people out to sea. The crew members were holding out their hands and hissing at the people to hurry up and get on board. The captain was already at the wheel. So this was it, thought Javed: this was the white ship, this was the white ship that would take them to Australia. When Javed looked back towards the shore he could just make out the four policemen, their trousers rolled up, submachine guns in their hands.

He was still asleep when the sun came up. During the night he had found a relatively comfortable position, half-resting his head on the shoulder of his neighbour. There was murmuring and movement: he opened his eyes. One portion of the sky was turning pink, the engine was still making its monotonous noise. Javed's biscuit had gone soggy, so he ate it. People were stirring, stretching their limbs: you could feel the boat gently rocking. Somewhere a baby was crying. There were shouts and arguments. Javed looked out at the horizon: it looked higher than the night before. Then he realised: the boat was sinking—the seat of his pants was wet, water was slowly seeping up through the planks. The captain began handing out buckets and tins, yelling at people to bail. Some next to Javed were already using their empty water bottles, cut in half, frantically throwing little cupfuls over the side.

Throughout the morning, the bailing buckets did the rounds of the men on board; it was late morning when Javed's turn came and the day was already hot. He was put below decks with another man of a similar age whose name was Shawali: they worked well together and soon had a good rhythm going, handing their full buckets up to the two men stationed above. Javed was grateful for the exercise; he said this to Shawali and he agreed. They speculated on how far they might have come in the night—the engine never stopped throbbing—and agreed they must be close to, perhaps only hours away from, Australia. They agreed they had made a good choice—Shawali even had a distant relative there, and this relative was always sending money back and praising his adopted home. Shawali was an engineer and he was quite sure, he told Javed, that in such a new country, with so much building to be done, he would soon find work.

When the bucket-carriers above called down that it was time to hand over to a new team, it was well past midday. Shawali led Javed to his spot below the wheelhouse on the starboard side and introduced him to his wife and young daughter. He took a plastic bag of food from a canvas pack and from that a ring-pull can of tuna and some bread: his wife spread them on a small cloth and invited Javed to eat. Javed was very hungry now—he picked out a chunk of tuna with his fingers and put it on some bread, felt a shiver of pleasure as he put it in his mouth. Shawali smiled and handed Javed an apple.

The two talked all afternoon but by evening they had run out of things to say. The sun was sinking, a big orange ball; Javed watched it go down. Shawali and his family shared the last of their bread. Javed was tired, the day had been long. He had already drunk all his water. He excused himself and with his bag for a pillow he curled up against the wheelhouse wall.

But he had not been sleeping long when a strange feeling woke him. Others were stirring too. The engine had stopped. One of the crew members came up from below and spoke quietly to the captain; the captain followed him back down. Now everyone was waking up, unsettled by the unfamiliar silence. The captain reappeared, looked up at the sky, then went inside the wheelhouse to check his equipment. A delegation of men approached the cabin window and started remonstrating with the captain, who, in his native tongue, told them to go away. But the men would not, and others pressed in around the window too. Then there was a shot and everyone ducked. The captain was waving a pistol, telling the troublemakers to back off; he had the situation under control, they would be in Australia soon.

They drifted all night and all the following day. There was no food and the only fresh water was in a plastic barrel that a delegated crew member guarded carefully, doling out small and ever-diminishing quantities. The bailing didn't stop. The heat was unbearable. Everyone started to get sick; a toilet had been improvised off the stern with a couple of planks and a curtain hung for privacy and, aside from the bailing, the only other sound was of liquid shit hitting the water.

The next day a plane flew overhead and circled

around; everyone shouted and waved, some people shook their orange life jackets over their heads, others held their children up high in the air for the plane to see. A crew member doused a rag with diesel fuel and lit it, then dropped it into a tin bucket from where a big column of black smoke rose into the air. The plane flew away.

Later that day the weather turned. A strong wind blew up from the south and waves crashed over the deck. Some of the parents tied their children down, to prevent them being washed away. The storm went on most of the night.

Next morning, far off, finally, a ship appeared, a navy ship to judge by its markings. It took a long while to assume its proper size. It came alongside, a rope ladder was lowered, and one by one they all made their way up.

Javed, I said, please eat. I held out a dry biscuit. His face hung heavy, his shoulders drooped; he had carried his burden so long he looked crushed. I will never eat, he said, until I see my wife and children again. But please, Javed, I said, I am a miracle worker, not a migration agent. Javed put his head in his hands.

He spent the next two years in his new home—khaki tents, razor wire, dripping taps, stinking toilets—on a speck of an island out in the blue. He was already a broken man when at last they said to him: You have been approved. They put him on a plane with twelve others and flew him to Brisbane airport, where a van was waiting out the front. He stared at the flat-roofed factories, lush vegetation, the houses with their big front yards. It was hard for him to remember if this was what he imagined when he'd imagined Australia; he had long put all dreaming, all wishing, all hoping from his mind.

They stayed a week at a volunteer's house—Welcome, welcome, said the woman, waddling down the drive—sleeping on mattresses spread across the floor. On the second night their host felt duty bound to let them know the reality of their situation. They were temporary residents only, she said. They could work, but their previous qualifications would not necessarily be recognised and their access to social-security payments was restricted. And no, said the woman, sadly, you will not see your families, you have no reunion rights. All this was relayed to the group via an interpreter, a short, thin man called Saed who seemed ashamed of every word.

The men talked among themselves that night and every night after, lying on their mattresses on the floor. Some were prepared to wait and see how the woman might help them, but others wanted to leave now. A brash young man called Ali told the group he had a brother-in-law in a town to the south: Haidar was his name, he had come out four years ago and found work in an abattoir. Ali was going down there, the others were welcome to join him, his brother-in-law would find them work for sure. Most argued against it: weren't they more likely to find jobs here, in the big city, than in the countryside far away? And it is not good to turn down hospitality when it is offered. Javed didn't especially like Ali, if anything he deeply distrusted him, but he could see he was a man of adventure: he would get him out of this cloying household and help him see what his new country had to offer. In the end, he was in the minority: of the thirteen arrivals, nine decided to stay in Brisbane and try to find work as taxi drivers, car washers, waiters. Only four, including Javed, followed Ali south.

They were given five hundred dollars each out of the host charity's coffers and a volunteer, Brad, a stout young man with a droning voice, offered to drive them as far as Sydney. From there they would take the train. Of the journey Javed remembered little: crossings, bridges, thinning suburbs, then the flatness going on forever. He knew he would have to understand that line out there, where the sky met the earth, if he were to get any kind of foothold in his new land. He'd need to get his heart out of the mountains, he told himself, his head out of the clouds: level himself out, stretch himself thin, find a voice that droned like Brad's.

From the old brick railway station, Ali led the odd little party down the town's main street to the pub. He told them to wait outside, then went inside to ask with few words and many gestures where the abattoir might be. Some men came out, all with glasses of beer in their hands, and each started giving directions. Eventually one of them took out his car keys and handed his glass to one of the others. Come on, he said to the visitors, I'll drop you there. They followed him around the corner to his ute. There was a dog in the back, tied to the roll bar. Don't worry about him, said the man. They all got in. A little way down the road the man stopped, got out and gestured for them to follow. They approached a big tin shed; there was a conversation at the side door, then all of a sudden their fellow countrymen were there; ten, a dozen men, all dressed in blood-smeared white coats with funny white hats on their heads. One of them pushed forward, tore off his rubber gloves and grabbed Ali in an embrace. The other men started cheering and clapping; they tore off their gloves too and began shaking the arrivals' hands.

The situation there was even better than the picture Ali had painted. The foreign workers were well respected, they had taken jobs no-one else wanted, and their boss had given them two big old houses to live in, out on the edge of town. When the end-of-work siren blew that day they all trooped off together down the road. Javed and the three others were given beds at Haidar's, a big old farmhouse surrounded by sheds and paddocks; you could see the other farmhouse in the distance. That evening a big fire was lit in the backyard and a goat roasted on a spit. There was singing and dancing, stories. It was late when they all went to bed.

Javed took his place in the slaughterhouse with a numb willingness. His first week's wage was no sooner earned than spent—and every week's wage after that. Haidar knew a *hawaladar*, a money dealer, back in Sydney, and every month via this *hawaladar* the men in the two houses would send their money home. This was the marker that gave measure to the days: every fortnight pay day, every month dreaming up a new password—*mountain, cloud, sky*—then giving it and the money to Haidar; then a few days after that the phone call to his wife (*Tell the dealer the password is appletree*). Then the same thing over again. Before he knew it, months had passed, and, before he knew it, a year.

Javed hated the abattoir, the moaning cattle, the endless slaughter, the dull thud of death. There was no sense of time passing in any meaningful way. When the new spring came he dug up a little patch of ground, spread it with manure and planted a handful of tomato seeds he had saved and dried. It was not so much to eat the summer crop—they had food enough—but for the simple pleasure of watching them grow. At the end of the day, in the twilit stillness, he would take his bucket and water the seedlings that were now pushing themselves up through the earth. The others in the house laughed, but Javed ignored them: he knew they were jealous. They too had come from farming families, stretching back through the generations, and like him they yearned to sow and reap. The weather warmed, his tomatoes grew, but even as he tied them to stakes and the little green globules swelled, he knew he would not see them ripen.

He had heard about other work. Some of the men had begun to talk about the fruit-picking trail to the west, where you could double your earnings. Haidar argued against it: why give up a job, a house, on the chance of making more money elsewhere? But Javed's mind was fixed. He packed his bag and with five others headed west. They got a lift with a truck driver as far as Wagga Wagga, then split and took separate lifts further west. Javed travelled with Sameer, a surly creature who spoke little and who ate the food he'd brought without sharing. They arrived in Mildura just before sunset and waited outside the post office. The others didn't arrive until three in the morning, by which time Javed and Sameer had been stared at by passers-by, harassed by teenagers and questioned by the police. They all walked to the river and found a park where they slept as best they could until the magpies woke them.

They found their way to a vineyard out of town and were no sooner through the gate than they were given a bucket and began bumping along on a trailer out towards the day's pick. The work was hard, the heat worse and the bucket took forever to fill, but when they retired to their hut at the end of the day they had to agree that, yes, they had earned more here in a day than they ever would in the abattoir.

Javed worked that place for three weeks, then another vineyard for two weeks after that. In February he was picking nectarines at Tooleybuc, then peaches down at Nyah. In early autumn there were wine grapes at Red Cliffs and Robinvale, in May and June oranges and mandarins back at Tooleybuc. Come winter and nothing to harvest he found work pruning, roaming back to Mildura in the north-west and down through Swan Hill and Echuca and the central vineyards near Avoca. In spring there was citrus again, then the first stone fruits of summer. At Swan Hill he had found a new *hawaladar* to help him transfer money home, and every month he would make the journey there with the cash he had earned. He locked himself in a phone box, rang his wife, gave her the new password—*mountainsky, rivergorge, highplain*—spoke briefly to his children, then stood weeping until someone told him to move.

Javed was earning more, but the travelling never stopped. And it was difficult to socialise: to pick the quota he had set himself each day he could not stop to talk.

He entered his own little world—eye, hand, bucket—and in the evening only ate and slept. He felt like a man sleepwalking. In every town there were well-meaning people lobbying on his and the others' behalf—to get full citizenship status, to be reunited with their families, to become genuine members of the community—but it always felt like a lot of talk. For all his advocates' good intentions Javed was still travelling like a hobo, a pack on his back, his clothes unwashed, his face and hands weathered and worn.

One summer he decided he'd had enough. He hitched a ride to Melbourne, met a young volunteer and slept on the lounge-room floor of his share house. He found a job driving taxis—he knew how to drive a tractor, a truck, but for this kind of driving he had to learn again. People abused him. One night two young men beat him senseless, robbed him of the little cash he had and smashed all the windows of the cab; he was not welcome here, they said, and should go back to where he came from. Javed had three broken ribs and was liable for the damage. Weeks went by, he couldn't work; he suffered nightmares and terrible headaches. One day he scribbled *Thank You* on the back of an old envelope and left.

He caught a train to the end of the line, jumped the platform without a ticket, then looked for a lift north. An old panel van picked him up. The driver was a wiry man with lank grey hair and a grizzled beard. His name was Mick. There was a can of bourbon and Coke clamped between his thighs. The inside of the van was full of rubbish, there was a thick layer of dust on the dashboard and a collection of birds' feathers stuck behind the rear-view mirror. Mick asked Javed where he was from and what had happened. Javed told him. This country's fucked, said Mick. Javed could not bring himself to nod.

Mick was going to Mildura for the grapes, as he did every year; Javed said he would go there with him. The usual work was waiting: the same bucket, the same grapes, the same pickers' hut, the same hard bed. Javed worked alongside Mick for a few days but then the sound of his voice started to grate. Javed knew he meant well, they all meant well, but in the end he was better off alone. He would work from first light to last, save every cent, go to the *hawaladar* in Swan Hill and give him the money, the password, make the phone call, clear his conscience for another month. But one day he stepped into the room at the back of the Swan Hill shop and saw that something had changed. The *hawaladar* could not help him, he said, the government was watching, they didn't like it, Javed would have to go to the bank.

He didn't want to go to the bank—there would be a thousand questions and he wouldn't have the answers. He walked to the edge of town until he came to a park and sat on a bench to think. Three young locals had followed him. While one stood sentry at the entrance to the park the other two cornered Javed, tore the pack from his shoulder and took out the bundle of cash.

They had not hurt him, at least, and he still had two hundred dollars, his living money, in his wallet. With a long stick he poked the pack out of the tree. He started walking out of town. He had no idea where he was going. He reached a river, crashed his way through the scrub along its bank and came out into an open paddock. He crossed this paddock, jumped a fence, crossed another. The river seemed to be chasing him; no sooner was Javed clear of it than there it was again. Occasionally out on the open ground he came across a shallow billabong, left behind long ago when the snaking river flooded, and beside one of these he made camp. He lit a fire, warmed a can of beans, filled his billy and put it on the coals.

He watched and waited for it to boil but then he heard footsteps approach. A farmer had raised the alarm. The policeman asked to see Javed's papers—It's just a routine check, he said—while the farmer and a younger cop looked on. Javed's papers were in order, but his English let him down. He thought they were taking him back to the camp. He turned and jumped into the billabong, thrashing his way out towards the middle. He couldn't swim: he had never been able to. The older policeman took off his jacket, gun belt and shoes, raised his eyebrows at his colleague, and dived in after.

It was a very sorry-looking Javed who was eventually dragged to shore. They started interrogating him again—Why did he run away? Where were his papers? It took Javed a while to prise the waterlogged wallet from his pocket and the wet document from that. The older policeman, now squeezing out his socks, shook his head and smiled. His colleague unfolded the document and examined it carefully; he nodded and handed it back. In words spoken too fast for Javed to properly understand he reminded him of his rights and obligations under Australian law. The farmer fetched a blanket from his car. Javed could stay there the night, he said, so long as he didn't frighten the sheep. The senior policeman gathered up his things, and the three picked their way back across the paddock.

Javed stoked the fire. Between two trees he strung a washing line and hung his clothes out to dry. He wrapped himself in the blanket. Everything in his wallet was wet. One by one he lay his papers, the money he'd hidden from the thieves and his precious family photographs out on the ground in the afternoon sun. That seemed like a good plan. He pulled the blanket around him, and, using a log for a pillow, lay down to sleep. By the time the clap of thunder woke him, the wind was already up; his papers, banknotes and photos were fluttering everywhere, up over the paddock and beyond the tree line. Then it rained. It belted down angrily out of the sky, hammering him and everything around. A flock of sheep looked on.

So you ended up with nothing, I said. Javed nodded. And now you have found yourself here, under this rotunda, in this municipal park, in this godforsaken one-horse town? Javed nodded again.

I rummaged in my pannier bags and took out an assortment of things: the rabbit foot, the bottle cap, the

Federation Penny; fenugreek for the gut, St John's Wort for the brain. The street was quiet: I danced and chanted. In time Javed got his colour back. My biggest challenge was to stop him shivering, so I could get the assuasives down.

But where will you go now? I asked. Home to the mountains, he said. *Home to the mountains?* What could I do? I could not get him permanent residence, a decent job, an English class, a family reunion, respect. I could not set him a place at our table. A quick trip to the Hindu Kush was beyond me. I saddled Murphy, refilled the hole.

We made a pretty sight: the Afghani, the donkey and me, clip-clopping up the winding road to the top of Mount Buangor, to take a look at the view. Javed sat side-saddle, like an old hand, flicking Murphy's rump. Up we went, up and up. He told me of his home in the mountains, his family, his friends. He told me the story of Nasrudin, smuggling donkeys over the border. We laughed, the best medicine of all. There was a lookout at the top; a bench seat, a picnic table and an information board. I gave Javed my prescription and left him to the view.

Was it wrong to leave him up there, high on that mountain peak? Should I not have brought him back down to the plains, to the patriots and the pedants, the little-minded enquiry officers, the form-filling, the sneering, the jeering, the hypocrites, the holier-than-thous? No. He will find time for his own down-going—Murphy and I, we were already out on the plain.

5

THE QUIET GIRL

I shouldn't have done that. Nine hundred and ninety metres above sea level, up a winding road, with an enthusiastic Afghani whipping your hide. Murphy knew it a moment of great import and gave it all he had but now that we were back in the lowlands, just the two of us, on those straight roads through the stubble fields towards the vanishing point, he had slowed to a snail's pace, wheezing and panting for breath. I slowed my pace to match. The distant markers—a tree, a ridge, a farm shed—took so long to come towards us we might have been moving backwards. I gathered some pellitory from the side of the road, made up a decoction and force-fed it to him. It's to ease your wheeze, I said.

The memorial at Joel Joel was our next stop, in a paddock at a junction of roads past Warrak, Ben Nevis and Crowlands. I hoped to find offerings there. We were already finding drier air: a powder-blue sky above and a powerful sun approaching its zenith. Murphy's coat had got up a sheen. I'm not sure what I would do if one day he lay down beside the road and died. Give him a kick, I suppose. But if he got so stubborn as to never move again—I mean never, ever again. What would I do then? Find another donkey? They say they run wild in the great deserts of the Interior; he is not so special as all that. But I have become fond of him, his sombre eyes, his mute expression, his slow, plodding ways. I doubt I could go on without him. It's true I've had carnal relations with him—as repugnant as this may be—but it's lonely out there on the road and the nights are often cold. In a duplicitous world Murphy's unvarnished simplicity has always been a source of comfort and warmth.

We travelled all day along a minor road that chased a gully north-west. The late-afternoon shadows lengthened, the dead gums lay themselves down in black: very solid, very precise. Murphy's footfall grew louder, the whole world grew louder, chattering its otherworldly noises before lights-out and sleep. It was almost brandy hour but I could not stop: I needed to make Joel Joel before nightfall. Murphy had other ideas. Like a dog accustomed to bringing its master his slippers as in the good old days many dogs did, with the lengthening shadows, the dancing gnats and the change in volume of the earth's myriad sounds, my beast thought evening was at hand. Soon his master would make camp for the night and soon take the weight from his back. He stopped; I poked him. If it were not in contravention of the laws of physics I would say he then stopped even more.

It was a while since I'd used the carrot and the stick: an old trick, tried and true. The former I hung from a second stick, on a piece of string, a couple of inches from his nose. This stick I held in my left hand, the whacking one in my right. Years of practice had made me very adept at manipulating these two sticks, like rubbing the tummy and patting the head. Shake, whack; shake, whack. This normally had the effect of moving Murphy forward a step or two, either in pursuit of the left hand's reward or in flight from the right hand's punishment, but could sometimes inexplicably leave him standing there while he made up his asinine mind. I want the carrot, he thought, with his own brand of donkey logic, but although, he went on, it is only inches from my nose I know that to get it I will need to make an extraordinary effort which it is not in my nature to make. But if I do not make this effort and get the carrot—and the carrot is very tempting, no doubt—then chances are my master will whack me and I will have to step forward anyway, if I am not to be whacked a second time.

The desire not to be whacked was as strong in Murphy as the desire to eat the carrot but neither, separately or in combination, was stronger than his desire to stand there and do nothing. It was natural in him. I could dangle the carrot in front of his nose and whack his arse from now until eternity but it would not change his ways. I have learned this much through my long association with him: each morning he will learn his idiocy anew. Damn, he will say to himself, feeling the stick on his rear again, someone is whacking me, I should move out of the way. And then: Now look, where did that come from, right there, in front of my nose, a nice juicy carrot, it's as if someone had put it there on purpose so I could have reason to get away from this stick. Then: Ouch! Someone is whacking me! Then: Look, a carrot! Then: Ouch! And so on. The day darkened, the stars came out, the moon hoisted itself into the sky. Step, stop; carrot, stick. Carrot, stick; step, stop.

It was late when I saw the headlights approach; I could not let any more time get away. I hailed down the truck and asked the driver if we could ride in the back. My name is Simpson, I said, and this here is my donkey, Murphy; we are on our way to the Sunset Country, then north, to the Inland Sea. A nervous, distraught-looking man, he said he could take us as far as Murtoa. He let down the ramp. Cattle had been in there, or sheep perhaps; it stank of manure, and damp straw was piled up in one corner and covered by a tarpaulin. He bolted the gate; we moved away. The road hummed. Murphy began braying, stretching his neck and flattening his ears. I tried to quieten him, fearing the driver would abandon us, but he only brayed all the louder. He has smelled the excrement, I thought, and become prey to some obscure animal lust. Then I saw the tarpaulin move. I bent down and pulled it back.

Her name is Laura, that's all I can get from her: a teenager, dark skin, full cheeks, a bloodshot look in her eyes. The driver was reluctant to part with her at first but in the end I bribed him with the few precious dollars I had. I said what was done was done and it was now between him and his God. He said he wasn't sure he had a God: I said he should find one. He asked where he might look and I told him in his heart. He did not understand. You could at least say sorry, I said. Sorry, said the man. A weaselly-looking thing with a grey goatee, flannel shirt and dirty jeans. The transaction concluded, he drove away. I tied the girl to Murphy's back and led her in off the highway to a picnic ground by a creek where I cleaned and dressed her wounds. Laura, she said, and fell silent again. I gave her a nettle and rosemary douche and a poultice of ragwort for the bruises. I harvested some horsetail from down by the creek and made a strong decoction from it. She suffered my ministrations uncomplainingly, like the patients I have dreamed about.

We stayed a week at Malakoff Creek. On the eighth day with Laura still wan we set off, she now riding side-saddle, me walking ahead with the rein. We travelled all day and as evening fell made our way to the hall at Navarre, an old fibro building with an elegant marble monument at its entrance. The key, as always, was under the mat. There was a musty smell inside and a mausoleum echo. Beneath the honour roll I made up a bed. On a bench in the kitchen off the main part of the hall the Navarrans had left tinned food, pickles, two bottles of brandy and half a dozen sad-looking carrots. I fed Murphy, ate some pickles, opened the brandy, drank.

Days passed. Then one evening, a visitor: glassy eyes and a putty nose. He was her brother, they needed to talk. He knelt beside her in the hall and put his ear to her lips. He said he was taking her home. Home? I asked. We left her sleeping, and sat together out on the step.

She rang me a fortnight ago, he said: scared. It had taken this long to track her down. They came from outback western New South Wales, a long way from here. A couple of years back Laura had got into trouble, stealing, so they put her in juvenile detention way down in Wagga Wagga but she fell in with a bad crowd there. She went to Newcastle, then up to Queensland. She found a boyfriend, an older fella, and lived with him out past Gympie. He was a motor mechanic; they lived out in the bush doing drugs, mostly pot, and whatever else came through. One night Laura tried to rob the roadhouse so they put her back in again. I'm just telling you, said the brother.

When she finally got out on conditional bail with assurances to every authority figure who sat down in front of her that she would return to her family, Laura now, he said, broke bail and hitched back to Newcastle where she stayed in a big share house on the edge of town. In the driveway was a car up on blocks, a kids' swing on the lawn. Laura had a bungalow—a shed, really—out the back and the twenty-three-year-old unemployed spray painter from Gosford who on her first visit there had his way with her had his way with her again. She had just turned fifteen. The bungalow was dank, with spiders in the corners, and Laura would lie on her back and watch them working their webs while the spray painter did what he wanted. The bungalow was very hot in summer; Laura put an old blanket up over the window and used an old fan she found in the hard rubbish to move the air around. Everyone was on the dole or doing piecework and there was always something going on with the cops, the courts, a parole officer or social worker, and these dramas made up most of the conversations around the table. Laura knew this was not her family, and if it was a community it was not a good one, but she had cut herself off so much from her real family, her real community, that she didn't know how to get back.

The brother found her in Newcastle and brought her

home but she had trouble settling. What are you scared of? he said. She said she wasn't scared of anything, she just needed a little time. This was the beginning of her quietness. She went back to school but she did no work; if a teacher asked her a question she would turn her head and look away, far away, past the middle distance to something beyond. The teachers called her parents in and they consulted a social worker who in turn called in a liaison officer; adults were moving at all angles around her, meeting, conferencing, splitting up, regrouping. She took up with a local man she met one day in the street, a miner, a scruffy-looking man ten years her senior. Against the protests of her parents, her brothers and her sisters she moved into his shack outside town. There was good money to be made at the mine but her boyfriend was hardly ever there; he had a greater liking for staying at home, sleeping in late, sitting outside the shack with a beer in his hand and throwing a stick for the dog. Laura spent most days doing the same.

One day a woman from welfare arrived, accompanied by a local policeman. While the policeman took the miner aside and gently reminded him about the laws governing the age of consent, the welfare officer sat with Laura and reminded her about her responsibilities to herself and her community. The visitors left. The dust had not even settled when the miner began hurling abuse, accusing her of lying to him about her age. Laura was indifferent. She did not love the miner, but she did not hate him either. The next morning they packed everything into the Commodore and drove south. They'll be back tomorrow, the miner said, and they'll want to take you from me. They drove all day, slept in the car and late the next day crossed the border into Victoria. He had a mate who worked in the cannery at Shepparton and this mate got him a three-day shift. They slept on a mattress on his lounge-room floor. Laura lazed around the house, wandered the streets, sat in the parks, did nothing. One day outside the supermarket an open, honest-faced woman asked was she all right. Laura looked at her for a moment and thought about answering but instead, like at school, looked away.

One night a couple of weeks after that the miner came home late. He was sleeping with a girl from the cannery. He told Laura this the next morning, straight out, thinking that by doing so he might get the upper hand. When he didn't come home again the following night, Laura crawled into bed with his friend, a big, awkward man who smelled of bacon and cigarettes. When she next saw the miner she hurled a bottle at his head, slammed the door and went to the pub and got drunk. Later she let a group of men take her to a spot down by the river and do whatever they liked. When they'd finished they dropped her out on the edge of town. She hitched a ride with a truck driver as far as Seymour where she slept under a picnic table until the sun woke her, then she walked to the roadhouse and asked around for a lift. The next driver tried to touch her; Laura started crying. He panicked and pushed her out at a roadside stop near Kilmore. She spent the rest of the morning sitting under a tree. Around lunchtime a car pulled in and a middle-aged couple got out to stretch their legs and dump some rubbish in the bin. The man got down on his haunches and asked could they do anything to help. His wife stood a little distance away. On the edge of the city near Campbellfield, Laura asked the husband to pull over. The woman thought she wanted to vomit and turned around to see, but Laura was already out walking. Are you all right? the man called after her. Leave her, Greg, the woman said.

Laura crossed the car park to Campbellfield Plaza. It was cool in there; people were wandering around, browsing the shops, eating their lunch. She sat on a mock-antique park bench and started to beg. People gave her a wide berth. Eventually a man came over and sat down beside her. He looked like a nice man, a tradesman, in his thirties. Dirty overalls and leather boots. His name was Niall. He gave her a five-dollar note and invited her to stay at his place, he had a spare bed, no strings attached. Back outside they threaded their way through the car park to his old Toyota tray truck with motorbike parts in the back. He had to clear the junk off the passenger-side seat before Laura could get in. His house was back off the highway, near Donnybrook. They followed a dirt road through rough, rocky paddocks to a brown-brick veneer sitting on its own in a paddock surrounded by other paddocks, with a big tin shed off to one side. There was a trail bike out the front and a petrol drum with a hand pump on top. Niall led Laura inside. It was a single man's house. He explained how his wife and kids were now living with a new bloke near Whittlesea. He showed her a picture of his eldest boy, blu-tacked to the fridge: he had a mullet just like his dad.

Niall had a single bed in the spare room with a teddy-bear mattress on it and he set Laura up in there.

That night he cooked a big pot of pasta and after the meal they sat outside in the warm still air, drinking cans. Niall said she didn't have to stay, he understood, but the room was hers if she wanted: better here, he said, than sleeping rough. Laura gave no answer to that but Niall guessed she had nowhere else to go. That night on her bed in Niall's spare room in the glow of moonlight from the curtain at the window Laura listened to the distant sound of cars on the freeway and, late, a goods train clattering past.

She spent a month there; Niall didn't touch her. He spent his days tinkering with his trail bike out in the yard and sometimes, suddenly, going off in his truck to 'do a job'. Laura slept in, wandered around half-dressed until lunchtime and in the afternoon watched television or Niall working on his bike. They usually had their first can about three. One day she said she was going into town; Niall dropped her off at Upfield Station, at the very end of the line. She came back late in the afternoon with cash and a sixpack. Niall didn't ask. She did the same thing a few days later, and twice the following week.

Then one day Laura said she had to leave. Niall told her he knew a bloke who did a run sometimes to the Mallee—maybe she could get a lift with him? A few days later a truck pulled up out the front. The sun was just up. Niall said goodbye to Laura still wearing his underpants and T-shirt and picking the sleep from his eye. They didn't touch. The truck drove off into the warm morning; Niall stood and watched it go.

It was a small cattle truck with a drop-down ramp on the passenger side. The driver, a thin, weaselly-looking man, was off to pick up some beef cattle from Murtoa. Laura knew from the moment she stepped up into the cabin that this would not be a free ride. He started saying things, filthy things, things Laura knew before the day was out she would have to submit herself to. *Why?* Because. *Why because?* He took out his mobile phone and spoke to his mates, and near Beaufort he turned off the highway and followed a road for ages until they came to a driveway marked by two white-painted tyres. Facing the road was an auction sign with weeds growing high around it and down the end of the driveway a farmhouse among a cluster of trees.

The truck pulled up outside the house. There were weeds here too, and cans strewn around the yard. The driver explained to Laura what was going to happen next but that she shouldn't worry, they would all chip in and give her some money after to help her get home. He walked around to the back of the house and reappeared, pushing the front door open from the inside. It had dropped on its hinges and had to be scraped across the floor. He stood on the front step and lit a cigarette. Soon two men in a white ute arrived. They greeted the truck driver, shook his hand, glancing up at Laura sitting in the cabin. From the back of the ute they took out two slabs and four bags of ice—they dragged a cut-down diesel drum out of the shed, smashed the ice into it and arranged the cans on top.

Later that afternoon the driver woke Laura and led her to a bedroom inside where a dirty mattress had been laid on the floor. What followed went on for a while and when it was over it was nearly dark. The men pulled another half-drum out of the shed and lit a fire in it. In the bedroom, Laura drifted off to sleep—a kind of wilful fainting. The men had thrown a blanket over her, she could feel the blood and whatever else seeping out onto the mattress. She curled herself into a ball. There was enough moonlight on the window to find its way through the blanket she had now drawn up over her head and when she blinked her eyes open this light looked blue, almost ocean blue, and seemed to swallow both her eyes and the room. She wanted to know what they'd left down there but couldn't bring herself to touch it.

Out in the yard, the talk was subdued. The three men were discussing what to do with her. One said they should leave her, she could find her own way home; another said they should drop her off in the nearest town; the third, the driver, said no, they had to get rid of her, he would take her out to the quarry on Readings Road. The others deferred to this, not least because it wiped their hands of it. They drank a little longer, not talking, then put Laura in the back of the truck and covered her up with a tarp.

Give her to me, said the brother: I want to take her home. Let me fix her first, I said. The brother said he didn't believe in me or my miracles and I said he should look me up in the history books where both were well attested. What history books? he said. I told him about Shrapnel Gully, the bullet in the heart, Lasseter's vial, the Inland Sea, the waterbirds wheeling and the shoals of silver fish shifting and breaking under a caramel moon. (Of course he believed in me: how else could he see me?) You must let me take her with me, I said: I will find the healing waters, bring her home renewed. People are always saying that, he said. He got up to leave; he said nothing else. I stood and watched the old station wagon go.

We set out soon after from that place, under an unforgiving sun. Broken roadside scrub, paddocks scraped clean by scraggy sheep, the creek gullies raw wounds, a horizon so low it seemed to hit you from behind. Laura now sat atop Murphy with an almost regal air, brushing away flies with a switch. She had gained weight, and Murphy sank noticeably further under it each day. We passed through Morrl Morrl, then followed the Wallaloo Creek gully north past Callawadda to Marnoo and on towards Rupanyup, where I had been well supplied in the past. The altar slab there is a granite block in the main street of the town. But there was nothing: no food, no money, no candle burning.

We removed to a camp on the outskirts where before a crackling fire I divided the last of the food. Laura ate hers in silence; I drank the last of the grog. *Thalassa! Thalassa! The Inland Sea!*—these are the words I rock myself to sleep with now, each exhausted night. The Inland Sea, Jack, the Inland Sea, one day you will find it and fill the vial, the jerry can, the drum; one day you will return with palm fronds waving to anoint the foreheads of the ill, the poor, the crippled and insane. All those struck down will be raised up.

Late next morning Murphy woke me. It felt like someone had pulled the curtains back on our dingy, firelit room; everything was flooded with air, space, light. It took me a while to take it all in: the roadside stop with its scrubby tree and concrete table was part of a much bigger landscape of sky, fields, road. Murphy was still tethered to a nearby sapling. The fire was still smouldering, a mound of grey ash. But Laura was gone.

I found her in the adjoining field. She had pushed through the barbed-wire fence and made a track through the grass which I followed until I came to a clearing with her lying in it. It was not until I'd sat her up that I saw she was bleeding again, red rivers down the insides of her thighs and a thick congealed puddle on the ground. Her face was livid; she fell into my arms. Laura? I said. I wiped away the muck and tied her to Murphy's back: a floppy, lifeless thing. No, I had not cured her, her wound was deeper than my quackery could ever know—a deep fissure, right down to the core. And now, what now? O fateful day that I found her in that truck!

I diverted to a nearby district hospital, one day's walk away, where a nurse had once been kind to me with a box of bootleg pethidine. But there were no cars, no people. Perhaps it had closed for the day? I stepped back and forth in front of the automatic doors until my head began to spin. I cupped my hands: down the corridor in the distance I could see the reception window but the shutter was down. No, I thought, this hospital has not closed for the day, or for that matter the week or the month; this hospital has closed for good.

Then the strangest thing. The sky darkened; there was a shrieking buzz, and the locusts hit. We took shelter in the doorway; I tried to prise open the glass doors but they were too strong or I was too weak or both, so I broke a window and crawled inside. I could hear the locusts screaming and the sound of them hitting the windows. I moved down the corridors, my feet scuffing the patina of dust. Back at the front door I pushed the green button but there was no power, so I smashed the glass with a chair. Murphy and Laura were where I had left them, Laura still limply clutching his mane. I whistled him up; he followed me inside.

6

THE FALLEN TEACHER

We made our way through the empty corridors and in a single-bed room in the sunniest wing I made us a kind of home. A strange little ménage. Eventually the locusts stopped. I attended to Laura with the things I had, then went searching through the building to see what else I could find: medicines, drugs, all the things I had desperately disbelieved. But everything had been taken. It was a dismal place, with a fetid smell of mould and damp, dog shit in the corridors and bird droppings on the walls.

In the very last room in the far south-west wing, to my surprise I found a sign of life. I heard what at first sounded like a low animal growl and imagined a pack of guard dogs grown hungry and wild, ready to rush out and attack me. But as I moved closer I recognised a few words, and the odour wafting down the corridor was also distinctly human: stale air, sweat and piss. Still, I was not prepared for the sight that greeted me when I put my head around the door.

He had certainly made himself at home. There was a bed made up with pillows, sheets and blankets. He'd also found himself a trolley tray, on which lay the scraps of a recently eaten meal. Strewn around the room were his possessions: junk to the amateur eye but to the gentleman in the bed undoubtedly all items of great value. The gentleman in the bed. It is difficult to paint a picture of him without resorting to caricature. He had a full beard, flecked with grey, and his wild hair reached past his shoulders. His eyes were both frightening and frightened. He looked me up and down—my tattered old military garb, the Red Cross brassard on my arm, toes sticking out of my trench-rotted boots. Where's your donkey? he said. In a room in the other wing, I said. I was hoping to meet the donkey too, said the man. Perhaps I will bring him around later, I said. Do you know how long I've been here? he asked. I said I couldn't guess. Two years, he said—he was, he said, in another room for a while but it was too bright and sunny in there. He spoke too loudly, as if to an audience. He was quite content, he said, he had everything he needed, whenever he got bored he would go for a walk in the grounds. But what is wrong with you? I asked. He had to think about this. Something had broken in his head, he said, a big rubber band as he liked to think of it that had been pulled too tight and then at some point had yielded: you could almost hear the thwack.

At first the marriage breakdown and divorce had, he said, failed to upset his equilibrium, believing as he did that the more stars you have in your eyes the longer it should take for the darkness to extinguish them. When at the age of twenty-eight he left the city to take up a teaching appointment in a nearby town he could hardly see the road, so many stars did he have. He settled into the little weatherboard school with the asphalt playground and gave himself to it, body and soul. He was much loved. He met, courted and married the local MP's daughter, herself a teacher, and together they bought a cottage in the centre of town from the front gate of which the soon-to-be-ex-teacher could wave and smile to the passing parents and children and bask in the warmth of their glow. It was all very nice. He felt that all was well with the world, that his country was a happy one and that he was lucky to be living in it, that his government was a beneficent one and his fellow citizens were honest, hard-working and selfless.

This was, he said, to him, now standing at the dirty window and looking out at the unpruned rose bushes, self-evident. As it should be. But, he continued, maybe it was precisely this seeming self-evidence that allowed us to be governed by what he liked to call The Great Delusion. Calling something white, he said, when it is quite clearly black or day when it is obviously night, trusting outward appearances and believing what you're told. Look at you, he said, turning to me: a nationalistic victory spun from abject defeat. There is always a certain amount of self-deceit necessary for the healthy maintenance of a society hell-bent on proving the sun shines out of its arse.

But, he continued, getting back into bed and pulling a blanket up to his chin, this growing awareness of The Great Delusion and the way it controls our lives was still a barely detectable light from a distant star when the newly married young man from the city settled down with his wife in their cottage in town. Then one day he took a letter from the box: they were closing down the school and terminating his position. The soon-to-be-ex-schoolteacher protested to the department and pleaded on behalf of his pupils, who would now have to travel half a day every day to get an education. Surely it was a bureaucratic error? He rallied the kids and their parents, raided the art-materials cupboard to make colourful placards and spent as many school hours as was practicable setting up photo opportunities for the local press and anyone else with a camera, including on one memorable occasion a photographer from a major metropolitan daily. After a week or so of this, some of the parents made arrangements for car-sharing to and from the larger school in the faraway town, some opted to school their children at home, the rest for anything other than a continued association with the former teacher who in their admittedly non-professional opinion was beginning to lose his marbles.

The ex-teacher kept vigil outside the school for months: a sign was hung along the fence, there was a fold-up table with a petition on it, a fire to keep him warm. The occasional passing tourist slowed down to look but, for the townspeople, the whole thing had become a huge embarrassment. He next tried a fundraising walk, had a slogan printed on a coloured singlet, put flyers in shop windows and harangued passers-by: fifty cents a kilometre, with all money raised going to a fund to reopen the school and ensure tenure of a qualified teacher. He became a familiar sight on the back roads of the region in his singlet, shorts and running shoes, walking all day and each night sleeping in a swag by the side of the road. His pace never slackened, slow and steady, nor his demeanour: his chest puffed out, his head held high, his forearms working like pistons. He lasted a couple of weeks; he had made almost nothing. He returned home in a dreadful state to his cottage and his wife but she didn't want to be his wife anymore. She stood in the doorway and wouldn't let him in. Further inside stood her father who the forlorn-looking amateur athlete now realised was behind her in a graver sense too. As a local MP his father-in-law could ill afford to have a lunatic son-in-law prone to public displays of his affliction, particularly if he was to advance his parliamentary prospects, as he wished to do. The ex-teacher's weeks out on the road had given the father the opportunity to speak to his daughter and help her see that her husband was a city boy who did not understand country ways. The daughter didn't need much convincing. By the time her soon-to-be-ex-husband returned she had already packed his suitcase—the suitcase he had brought all his hopes from the city in—and handed it to him around the flywire door.

The ex-teacher and now ex-husband maintained his vigil outside the school every day after that, including weekends. The grounds had become overgrown with weeds and vandals (his ex-students) had smashed all the windows and burned down the outside toilets. Then the weather turned. He shivered in front of a smoky fire and slept in the shelter of the portico wrapped in a blanket. He came down with a fever but would still not let go. What was he holding on to?

The father-in-law came around to present the divorce papers and the ex-teacher took them numbly from him. The father-in-law suggested he go back to the city, re-establish old contacts—but the ex-teacher wasn't listening. He began to really lose his mind, if he had not already lost it. With a belt he tied to his head a pillow that a kindly townsperson had given him, and at regular intervals banged it against a nearby lamppost, an act he insisted was symbolic but which was lost on a town unused to calling a spade anything but a spade. One night while he slept a group of ex-students—among them a kid called Rowan, whom the ex-teacher had worked hard on and held such high hopes for—dowsed him in petrol and set him alight. They let him writhe and roll before the leader unzipped his fly and pissed long enough to put him out.

He was taken to the hospital in a critical condition and, once out of danger, transferred from the intensive-care unit to a four-bed ward in the south-west wing. There was only one other patient there, an elderly man who spent most of the time sleeping. The nurses were certainly kinder than anyone else had been over the previous months and it would be no exaggeration to say that in their care in this quiet room of the hospital, with only a sleeping geriatric to unsettle his privacy, the ex-teacher found some personal happiness. No-one came to visit him: he didn't expect them to. This gave him a great sense of freedom in relation to his recent past; he may be a madman, he said, but at least he was a madman with a room, a bed and a retinue of helpers. In short, he felt well—but this did not prepare him for the shock of them telling him he was. Well enough, they said, to be discharged and to return once a week as an outpatient only. He followed the nurse down the corridor to the outside world but only a short way down the road he took out the secreted bottle of cleaning fluid, unscrewed the cap and drank.

He went straight back into intensive care, and then back to the south-west ward (his elderly room-mate hadn't noticed his absence). When he was discharged the next time he used a glass shard to slash his wrists, the next to drink the cleaning fluid that had served him so well the first. Now, when he was better in body, they concluded that he was not well in mind and put him in the new psychiatric ward (like the other wards but with a lockable door), which the patient was bold enough to assume had been built especially for him.

If he was happy in the other ward he was *very* happy here. He had his own television, his own around-the-clock nurse, and was allowed, accompanied by her, to take relaxing walks in the grounds. There was something very comforting knowing that people who thought you were crazy could treat you as such in an institution purpose-built for it. A whole section of a ward in a relatively small country hospital had been set aside to keep the ex-teacher off the street, a gesture he acknowledged with a good deal of humility. He gave the nurses no trouble, did as he was told and lived quietly within the routine they had laid out for him. It struck him that for all his previous bitterness towards the evils of free-market economics, government indifference and a perennially languid electorate, here was an instance of compassion at work. It might even have cured him, had the news not then filtered through the locked door of the psychiatric ward that permanent closure of the hospital was imminent. Apparently not so many people were getting sick and those who were might be better cared for in a large hospital a half-day's drive away.

The district hospital would be demolished and a new service station and roadhouse built in its place. No-one mentioned the well-regarded rumours that the ex-teacher's ex-father-in-law was the man behind this scheme. Files were packed, inventories made, patients forewarned. Some were transferred, while those unlikely to die in the immediate future were sent home to be cared for by family and once a week by a visiting nurse. As for the single patient luxuriating in the psychiatric ward, a quick appraisal by a consultant psychiatrist appointed by the hospital's advisory board deemed it in his best interests to return to society and be allowed to make an active contribution to it. An outpatient counselling service would be provided (weekly visits to the home of a local woman who had completed a social-work course by correspondence), to be supplemented by the bag full of pills and repeat prescriptions they gave him on discharge. The hospital was locked and barred, a wire-mesh fence was put up around it and guard dogs hired to roam the corridors at night.

When the first lot of dogs died no-one seemed particularly concerned, except the owner of the security firm who provided them. Perhaps they'd simply eaten something they shouldn't? But when their replacements fell over frothing too, people suspected foul play. The security firm pushed for compensation and, when it was not forthcoming, tried to pursue the still-mysterious owners of the hospital site through the courts. A new security firm was hired, a new set of dogs fell over dead, and when their replacements met the same fate a new court battle ensued. It was becoming clear that the decision to close the hospital and sell the land to a consortium, which may or may not be traced back to the ex-teacher's ex-father-in-law, had left a paper trail so labyrinthine that no small-security-firm lawyer, let alone the great Theseus, could find a way through it.

This time the dogs were not replaced, the perimeter fence was packed away and the building left to languish.

Vandals (the ex-teacher's ex-students, again) had some fun for a while but it wasn't long before they outgrew their delinquency and left town for the big city lights. The ex-teacher came in out of the cold and returned to the room which held so many happy memories for him: the flowering gum outside the window, the way the sunlight fell across his bed in the morning, the way the twilight coloured the walls. He liked the sounds: the currawongs in the trees, the distant noise of cars and trucks gearing down through town. The rooms and corridors were now his own, as were the grounds where he could wander for hours. He stored up packaged food from his brief trips to town and what he didn't need he went without.

The room had darkened; already it was late afternoon. Listening to the man's story it did strike me for a moment that someone who could so eloquently describe the reasons for his derangement might not be so deranged after all. But one glance gave the lie to that. He'd been talking too fast, in a kind of jabber, and had spat all over his beard which was now wet from the lower lip to below the chin. His eyes were white opals, glaring out from under a furrowed brow. His face was red, almost purple.

So, what now? I asked. I'll need to go to the cupboard, he said. I had no idea what he was talking about. But surely you can't stay here forever? I said. He assured me that, while forever was a long time, he would certainly be staying indefinitely. It was now common knowledge that his ex-father-in-law, the MP, had lobbied for closure of the school and the hospital and bought both properties via a network of offshore shelf companies and that until the courts untangled this deceitful web and the ongoing parliamentary inquiry was completed the building was the ex-teacher's to roam in as he wished.

He threw the blankets back and got out of bed. Aside from a thick hooded jacket all he had on were unsightly yellow walking shorts and a dirty pair of socks. So you see how my story fits, he said, into the story of The Great Delusion? Of how someone who believed in Universal Ideals was left standing in The Slough of Despond? I am the sickness and you are the cure, he said. I nodded. So, said the strange and hirsute gentleman: what cure will you use?

Now I saw where the conversation had been heading and where by the long road it had taken us. I explained how I had left Fowlers' stable twenty-six days ago, had been waylaid by a number of complicated healings since and was now being waylaid again; that my powers had been fading fast these past few years and that unless I found the water and filled the vial (I took it out of my shirt to show him) it would be all over with this myth, and so far as I could tell there was no other worthy waiting in the wings; that I feared the public trust in me was waning; that my donkey, faithful companion of this life and the previous, had become pneumonic and would be lucky to last another month, and that given the public's long-standing faith in us as a double act I could hardly go on without him; that I already had a patient in the other wing who was, so to speak, ahead of him in the queue and who, besides, had barely responded to my ministrations so far. In short, I said, to the ex-teacher standing by the bed with an air of knowing superiority, I am not the intercessor I once was. The ex-teacher smiled a madman's smile: Well then, he said, come with me.

He led me to a wing I'd not yet explored, down a short corridor to a door at the end. He opened it, reached around inside and took out a candle which he lit with a match from a box in his jacket pocket. By the light of this candle we entered what had once been a storeroom;

there were rows of grey metal shelves along the wall, all empty, some open cupboards, and here and there piles of flattened cardboard boxes on the floor. The ex-teacher led me further inside, to a cupboard at the far end. It had a warning sign on it. The ex-teacher yanked open its doors. This is the ward I used to be in, he said, and this is the cupboard they forgot to empty. Anamorph, Aropax, Biodone, Capadex, Largactil, Lithicarb, Luvox, Melleril, Paxil, Prozac, Serenace, Seroquel, Zoloft, Zydol. While he recited this fourteen-footed pharmaceutical litany, with his free hand he selected several packets and gave them to me. This is what we use now, he said.

I walked back down the corridor towards the sunny wing, the pills rattling in my pockets like matches in the hands of a pyromaniac. Laura was awake, sitting up on her makeshift bed staring at the wall; Murphy was standing asleep by the window in a posture of complete resignation. He had soiled the floor beneath him and the air was thick with the smell. I don't think Laura had even noticed me gone. Listen, I said, it's true: I am a quack. Whatever powers I once had have faded, I can do nothing for you; I have failed you, we have failed you; soon we make our last push inland to execute *more majorum* our ridiculous yet heroic death, and this we must do alone. I cannot take you with me. Here. I sorted through the pills, gave her some of the green and white ones and some water to wash them down. For myself I took a handful of every colour, so as to leave no stone unturned.

I sat cross-legged in the corner watching the light in the windows change. The room darkened, or the universe lightened, one can never be sure. Murphy became a shadow of himself or he the simulacrum of his shadow. It went on like this well into the evening. I felt a great burden fall from me. I began to rock like a baby and there was the sound of sloshing water in my head. At some point, on a line that I clearly saw extended into eternity, my eyes closed and behind them my indivisible mind drifted in a sea of black.

7

THE DESERT AND THE END

I was unhinged for a week and suffered the most bewildering hallucinations. I was Asclepius, then Hippocrates; a witch doctor, then a voodoo priest; my healer's staff became a jester's bauble in the court of an ailing king. Not since I first smoked opium in Egypt have I experienced such intoxication. At one point I was overcome by a bright cyan light. Through this light and out the other side I found myself on the steps of a temple riding a donkey that was not Murphy but at the same time somehow was, while at the top of these steps a priest in robes of green and gold beckoned me forward. I dismounted the animal, mounted the steps and followed this priest through the corridors and rooms until we reached an inner chamber where the walls were hung with tapestries of gold, studded with emerald and jade. On a throne at the far end of this room sat the High Priest, a green cape on his shoulders and a gold crown on his head. He reminded me of a cricketer I had once seen. Where are you going? he asked. To the future, I said. How long have you been travelling? Nearly a hundred years, I said. A piss in a bucket, said the High Priest. He summoned my guide forward and handed him a scroll, and the guide handed it to me. A map to the future, said the High Priest. He dismissed me and I followed the other priest back to my donkey, which had transformed into a lamb. I could not ride it, it was too small and weak, but this ewe-lamb then revealed itself to be possessed of human speech and willing to carry me. Jump on, it said. With the High Priest's map for guidance the lamb and I set off, but a hot wind blew and picked me up and raced me back across the desert and dumped me in the hospital room where I found myself sitting cross-legged in the corner again.

The sun sliced its way down the wall each day, crossed the floor and slid away into night. I didn't move, nor did Laura or Murphy, a mountain of manure beneath him. I worked my way alphabetically through the pills then, delirious and barely able to walk, went back to see my supplier for more. But my supplier was gone. I went to the cupboard in the storeroom but aside from a packet of Panadol and a couple of ampoules of morphine he had taken the lot. I drank a little morphine and let it take hold. I got Laura up and helped her wash. We're off, I said, as if it were a Boxing Day down the beach. I whistled Murphy up and an eyeball moved: through his mottled coat you could see the rib cage, there were tracks of dried snot from his nostrils, blowflies had made camp in the hive of his rear. When he finally found me within the range of his vision and got his rheumy eyes to focus it was a forlorn and defeated look he gave. But what could I do? He is my beast of burden, that is his purpose on this earth. I held a bent ear straight and whispered in it: We have not finished our business, mule, until the holy water is in the stoup.

I lifted Laura onto his back (his knees shivered), drank some brandy for strength, said goodbye to our hospital home and this time set off in an arc north-east. We went to the soldier on the plinth at Watchem, to the gates at Curyo, to the memorial in the main street of Rainbow: nothing, nothing, nothing. We turned south, closing a circle that had taken weeks to describe and which now brought us almost back where we started. We shuffled our way down the Avenue of Honour into Jeparit to try the Lone Pine there. But as soon as I started digging I knew it had been dug. I drank the last ampoule of morphine. *Have I done all I can? Did I leave some small thread hanging? What will be the final account?*

I led us boldly inland (It won't be long, Laura, I said) but we missed the Sunset Country completely and ended up in the Little Desert, south of Nhill. A stark, inhospitable place. I pulled out my maps in utter despair, for I could not find myself on them. Is it possible to disappear suddenly and completely from the face of the earth? Squat trees, dry grass, grey dust and sand; we lurched from one useless landmark to the next. Flies hovered in clouds above us, Murphy's wheeze was a broken accordion. I unloaded the pannier bags of all their things. O false apothecary! Laura watched, silently. *Who is she? Why will she not speak?* While beneath her poor Murphy my tender ass scrapes the sand with each weary step, heavy head, worn crupper, red welts on his withering withers. What happened to my light-footed little Platero, prancing in the butterfly fields?

The next morning Laura was gone, a fine layer of dust on her bed-roll. Murphy brayed like a wild beast until the sun was high. At the base of the tree under which I'd slept I started to dig, convinced that in some other time I had buried a bottle of brandy there, then even more convinced that this bottle of brandy was the Inland Sea I had been looking for and that by finding it and drinking from it all would be well again. But it was the wrong tree, it must have been; with Laura's switch for a divining rod I lurched from one tree to the next. *You have got through the difficult business, now you have only to dig.* Ravens wheeled above. The switch quivered ceaselessly in every direction but it was not until I'd dug a dozen fruitless holes that I realised it quivered not for water or liquor but because of my trembling hands. I tried to still them but couldn't. In the end I hurled it from me and saw it slither into the grass.

I dreamed I was back in Shrapnel Gully, the nation-making hellhole, working the track, ducking the sniper fire: *tweet!* then a *ping* or a *thump*. I bring down a widow, a disabled, a refugee, an addict, an orphan. All that. But at the beach the generals are barking at me to take them back where I found them: *We don't do that anymore.* I walk them all back up the hill and hide them in a trench so that no-one will see and I won't have to explain it later. When I open my eyes I see Laura, come back in from the desert. She is carrying mallee-root water in an old soft-drink bottle; in a grass basket there are broom ballart cherries, geebung drupes, quandong with sugarwood sap. She comes and goes over the days that follow, bringing food, healing plants, water. She makes a rough shelter and sets me up inside while she sleeps outside by a smoky fire under the stars. I am consumed by fever. Clearly I am in the last of my days. I look out at a diminishing world through crusty half-closed eyes. One day I see Javed the Afghan cameleer coming out of the desert towards me, behind him in the distance a shimmering mirage and all the wild donkeys herding at its shores to drink.

When Murphy finally collapses, felled as if shot, I ask Laura to help me to him. I lie with my head on his belly and listen to the faint gurgling inside. After a while it stops. Laura puts a poultice on my head. I'm sorry, I say. (I said I would bring her back home to her brother and I have not kept my word.) She says nothing. I ask for the Horne book—it's with my things—and on the palimpsest of *The Lucky Country* I make my final account. When

I'm done I ask her to bury it in the hole. She stands above me, book in hand, dark against the fulgent light. And now, I say: what now? Who's left to help and heal? Laura says nothing, buries the book, brushes the ground with her foot.

ACKNOWLEDGMENTS

Peter Cochrane's *Simpson and the Donkey: The Making of a Legend* (MUP, 1992) was an initial inspiration for, and an important resource during, the writing of this book.

Thanks to Kevin Pearson at Black Pepper for his early support and to Melanie Ostell for her help in guiding the text to its final incarnation. An earlier, much shorter version of this story appeared in *Westerly*, Vol. 46, November 2001.